Max's mind flew to the day he'd met Kate at a pool party at a friend's house.

She'd worn a green bikini that matched her eyes. But though her looks were what had caught his attention, it was her personality that had hooked his heart. Sweet. Fearless. Funny. In one short conversation she'd made him forget every other woman he knew. And now she was here. In front of him.

His heart stumbled. His knees weakened.

But when she realized who'd tapped her the happily surprised expression on her face crumbled and was replaced by something Max could only describe as a look of horror.

"Max!"

A lump of emotion lodged in his throat. More of their life together flashed through his brain. The way they'd talked till dawn the day of the pool party. The first time they'd kissed. The first time they'd made love. Their wedding day.

He'd thrown it all away.

Dear Reader

Max Montgomery was a rich kid, a lucky guy who had everything. Good looks. Personality. Money. His life was perfect until he went to work for the family business, Montgomery Development, and discovered his dad was a bit of a scoundrel.

But he got lucky again and found the love of his life: Kate. And Kate kept him grounded—until Max stumbled on the big family secret. That secret shook him so badly he started drinking. He drank so much he ruined his sterling reputation and ended his perfect marriage.

Almost a decade later his father is dead, Max is sober, and he wants his wife back. The only problem is she also has a secret. She was pregnant when she left, and he has an eight-year-old daughter he's never met.

Suddenly the shoe is on the other foot. Kate doesn't just have to forgive him; he has to forgive her too.

Forgiveness is a funny thing. Real love is even more intriguing. I learned a lot about life and people while writing this story. Sometimes I laughed. Sometimes I cried. But with Max and Kate there was never a dull moment.

I think you're really going to like this one.

Susan Meier

First Time Dads!

From bacherlorhood to fatherhood

THE TYCOON'S SECRET DAUGHTER
September 2012

NANNY FOR THE MILLIONAIRE'S TWINS
October 2012

THE TYCOON'S SECRET DAUGHTER

BY
SUSAN MEIER

First published in Great Britain 2012
by Mills & Boon, an imprint of Harlequin (UK) Limited.
Harlequin (UK) Limited, Eton House, 18-24 Paradise Road,
Richmond, Surrey TW9 1SR

© Linda Susan Meier 2012

ISBN: 978 0 263 22796 3

Susan Meier spent most of her twenties thinking she was a job-hopper—until she began to write and realised everything that had come before was only research! One of eleven children, with twenty-four nieces and nephews and three kids of her own, Susan has had plenty of real-life experience watching romance blossom in unexpected ways. She lives in western Pennsylvania with her wonderful husband Mike, three children, and two over-fed, well-cuddled cats, Sophie and Fluffy. You can visit Susan's website at www.susanmeier.com

Books by Susan Meier:

THE BABY PROJECT*
SECOND CHANCE BABY*
BABY ON THE RANCH*
KISSES ON HER CHRISTMAS LIST

**Babies in the Boardroom* trilogy

For my friend, Denise.
The last idea we brainstormed together.
I'm sorry you couldn't see the finished book.

CHAPTER ONE

EXITING THE ELEVATOR in the lobby of Mercy General Hospital, Max Montgomery glanced up and did a double-take. The woman leaving the coffee shop looked exactly like his ex-wife.

As petite as Kate, wearing blue jeans and a little flowered top that was her style, with thick, shoulder-length sable-colored hair that swung when she moved, she had to be Kate.

He shook his head, telling himself that was nuts. His wife had left Pine Ward, Pennsylvania, almost eight years ago and he hadn't seen her since. She'd divorced him through lawyers. Hadn't answered the letters he'd sent to her parents' home. Hadn't even returned to visit as far as he knew. Not even at holidays. That couldn't be her.

He made his way to the glass exit doors and they automatically parted, but curiosity turned him around before he could step out.

The woman now stood in front of the elevator he'd exited, her back to him.

Sensation vibrated through him, the radar he'd always had with her. He'd always known when she was within twenty feet. Always known when she was about to walk into the room. Always known.

It had to be her. The radar never failed.

He took a few cautious steps toward her, but stopped. Even

if it was her, why would she want to see him? What would he say? Sorry I screwed up our marriage, but I'm sober now?

Actually, that wasn't such a bad idea. Of all the people on his twelve-step list, people he needed to make amends with, he'd contacted everyone but her. The person who most deserved his apology.

If it wasn't her, he'd simply apologize for the mistake.

Either way, he'd be apologizing. No big deal.

He sucked in a breath, crossed the small space between them and tapped her shoulder.

She turned.

His heart stopped then sped up again. It was her.

His mind flew to the day he'd met her at a pool party at a friend's house. She'd worn a green bikini that matched her eyes. But though her looks had been what caught his attention, it was her personality that had hooked his heart. Sweet. Fearless. Funny. In one short conversation, she'd made him forget every other woman he knew. And now she was here. In front of him.

His heart stumbled. His knees weakened.

But when she realized who'd tapped her, the happily surprised expression on her face crumbled and was replaced by something Max could only describe as a look of horror.

"Max!"

A lump of emotion lodged in his throat. More of their life together flashed through his brain. The way they'd talked till dawn the night of the pool party. The first time they'd kissed. The first time they'd made love. Their wedding day.

He'd thrown it all away for the contents of a bottle.

He cleared his throat. "Kate."

She motioned with her coffee. "I…um…I need to get this up to my mom."

This time when his heart up-ended it was with fear for her. "Your mom is here? As a patient?"

"No. No. She's fine." She glanced around nervously. "Daddy had a stroke."

Was that any better? "Oh, my God. I'm sorry."

"He's okay." She looked to the right again. "The stroke was reasonably mild. Prognosis is good." She tried to smile. "I've really gotta go."

It was the worst moment of his life. Eight years ago, she would have turned to him in this kind of tragedy. Today, she couldn't stand to be around him. In some respects, he didn't blame her. But he'd changed. He'd been in Alcoholics Anonymous for seven years. He was sober. And he did realize what he'd lost. But more than that, apologizing, admitting his faults, was part of his twelve-step program.

When the elevator pinged, he caught her arm to prevent her from turning. Electricity crackled through him.

Their gazes caught. His heart swelled with misery. God, how he'd loved her.

She swallowed. "I've really gotta…"

"Go. I know. But I need a minute."

Hospital employees walked out of the elevators behind them. The gathering crowd waiting for the elevator loaded inside.

She glanced around nervously.

Pain skittered through him. She couldn't even stand to be seen with him. He thought back to the times he'd embarrassed her and the pain became a familiar ache. He'd disappointed so many people.

But that was seven years ago.

And today was today.

He pulled her a few feet away from the elevators. "I have to tell you that I'm sorry."

Her face scrunched with confusion. "Have to?"

"Yes. It's part of the program."

Her eyes lit with recognition. "Oh, twelve steps."

"Yes."

She looked at him differently now, closely. "You're sober."

He finally let himself smile. He'd wanted to be able to tell her that for seven long years. "Yes."

Her voice softened. "I'm so glad."

His chest loosened a bit. Breathing became easier. "I am, too."

An awkward silence stretched between them. He understood. There really wasn't anything for them to say. He'd ruined their marriage. She'd left him to save herself.

She showed him the two cups of coffee again. "I should get this to my mom before it gets cold."

Pain radiated out from his heart to his entire body. He'd had this woman. She'd loved him and he'd loved her. She'd been everything to him and he'd driven her away.

Don't dwell on the past. Focus on the future.

He stepped back. "Yeah. Sure. I'm sorry."

The bell for the second elevator pinged. The doors swooshed open. Kate turned to get inside, but a little girl raced out.

"Mom! Grandma sent me to find you. She thinks you're making that coffee."

Mom?

His knees that had already been weakened began to shake. The little girl's hair might have been the same sable color as Kate's, but those blue eyes…they were Montgomery eyes.

Pain morphed into shock. Could this be his child? His daughter?

"And who is this?"

Kate's gaze flicked to his. Her hand fell protectively to the little girl's shoulder. "This is Trisha."

His body went stock-still. "Short for Patricia?" His beloved grandmother's name? Why name the little girl after his grandmother if she wasn't his?

She smiled weakly. Her eyes filled with tears. She whispered, "Yes."

Damn it.

He had a child. A daughter. And Kate had kept her from him?

He looked at the little girl again. Pain, wonder, curiosity simultaneously burst inside him. Everything in him wanted to touch her. To examine her. To see the beautiful child he'd made.

But anger warred with longing and both of them were wrapped in confusion. Was this why she'd left him? Because she was pregnant? Because she didn't want him to know his child?

Fury rose, hot and eager for release, but thank God his common sense had not deserted him. With this beautiful little girl standing so sweetly innocent in front of him, he couldn't out-and-out ask Kate if this was his daughter.

Kate wanted to grab her baby girl and run away. Not because she feared Max. When he was sober, he was a great guy. And right now he was sober. But drunk? He had never hurt her, but he'd ranted and raved, smashed dishes, broken windows. The night she'd made the choice to leave rather than tell him she was pregnant, he'd smashed their television and thrown a vase through their front window. She'd known she couldn't bring a child into that world.

But she'd also realized it wouldn't be good enough to merely leave him. He had money. He had power. After she had their baby, he'd get visitation, and she wouldn't be able to control what happened. If he drank around their little girl, or drove drunk with her in the car, he could kill her. And there would be nothing she could do to stop it, if only because every judge in the county owed his election to the Montgomerys.

That frightening night, standing amid the evidence that

his bad behavior was escalating, she'd made the only choice she could make. She'd disappeared.

She swallowed, motioned to the elevator. "We've gotta go."

He hesitated. His gaze slid to their daughter, then returned to her. "Okay."

She saw the anger in his eyes, and quickly herded Trisha into the elevator. The doors swished closed. Her eyes drifted shut, and she expelled a low breath as guilt trembled through her. She had no idea how long he'd been sober. Her parents didn't travel in his social circle and she lived too far away to hear a rumor.

What if he'd stopped drinking the day after she'd left? What if she'd kept Trisha away from him for nothing?

"Who was that?"

She opened her eyes to glance down at her daughter. This was neither the time nor the place to tell Trisha that she'd just seen her father, but she knew the time and place were coming soon.

The elevator doors opened. "Let's go. Grandma's waiting for her coffee."

Trisha giggled. "I know. She thinks you're making it."

Kate smiled at her lovely, innocent daughter whose world was about to be turned upside down, and headed to her dad's room. His "incident" had been a few days before. He was awake now, at therapy a good percentage of the day and so eager to get home he was gruff.

"Hey, Daddy." She leaned in and bussed a kiss on his cheek. "If I'd known you were awake I'd have brought you coffee, too."

Her mom stepped from behind the privacy curtain surrounding the bed. As tall as Kate, dressed in jeans and a sleeveless top, with her brown hair cut in a neat short style, Bev Hunter said, "He doesn't get coffee until the doctor says so."

Her dad rolled his eyes for Kate, but smiled at his wife. His words were slow and shaky when he said, "Yes, warden."

Kate's hands were every bit as shaky when she gave one of the two coffees to her mom. "Here."

"Thanks." Bev popped the lid, took a sip. "You were gone so long I worried that you'd gotten lost."

"Not lost."

"Mommy was talking to a guy."

Bev's eyebrows waggled. "Reeea-lly?"

"He wasn't somebody I wanted to see." She nudged her head in Trisha's direction. "But this isn't the time to talk about it."

Her mom frowned, then her eyes widened in recognition. "You didn't?"

"I didn't do anything. He just suddenly appeared out of nowhere. But July is the month Montgomery Development does their annual physicals." She squeezed her eyes shut. "I should have remembered that."

Her mom groaned. "So he was here, and he saw Trisha."

Kate grabbed a paper cup from her dad's tray table and handed it to Trisha. "Would you throw this away in the bathroom trash can and then wash your hands?"

Trisha nodded eagerly like the well-behaved almost-seven-year-old that she was. When she was gone, Kate said, "I have about thirty seconds. So just let me say Max found me. Trisha came out of the elevator when we were talking. He took one look at her and knew."

Her mom pressed her hand to her chest. "I knew you shouldn't have come home!"

"I wasn't about to desert the two of you when Daddy was so sick." She squeezed her eyes shut. "Mom, Max is sober."

Bev took a second to process that, then snorted in disgust. "And you're feeling guilty?" She snorted again. "The man had become violent and was getting worse by the day. You had no choice but to protect your child."

"But I could have checked on him—"

"You have no idea when he got sober. For all you know, he just went to his first AA meeting last week. This isn't the time to be second-guessing."

Kate heaved out a sigh. "Okay, but I know Max was angry. If I don't go talk to him, he'll probably come to the house tonight. Or I'll be hit with some kind of legal papers tomorrow. Or maybe both."

Walking out of the bathroom, sweet, trusting, Trish smiled. Kate's heart sank. If he came to the house, they'd have to have their talk in front of Trisha. And she didn't want Trisha to hear her dad was a drunk. Especially when she was too young to understand.

"You know what? I think I'd better deal with this now." She faced her mom. "Will you guys be okay for an hour or so without me?"

Her eyes filled with worry, Bev said, "Sure."

Kate sucked in a breath and turned to her daughter. "You behave for Grandma."

Trisha nodded and Kate left her dad's hospital room. She got into her car and drove to downtown Pine Ward. The small city was old and working to revive itself after the loss of the steel mills in the 1990s. Buildings from the 1940s were being renovated. Trees had been planted along the sidewalk on Main Street. A few new restaurants had even popped up.

She left her car in a parking garage and headed out. A couple of blocks and two turns took her off the beaten path to the place in the city where the newer, more modern structures stood. She stopped in front of the yellow brick building housing Montgomery Real Estate and Development. Only four stories, it nonetheless had an air of wealth and power. Quiet. Dignified. Understated.

She hesitated. Though Max had been reasonably calm at the hospital, she knew he was angry with her. He had to be. If the tables were turned, she'd be furious with him. So his anger was justified. And she had to admit that.

Maybe it would be better to give him a day or two to get past that? To get his bearings?

Blowing her breath out on a long sigh, she told herself no. If she didn't meet with him on her terms, they'd meet on his. He'd either come to the house and they'd fight in front of Trisha, or they'd meet in a room filled with lawyers. And she'd really lose because he could afford much better lawyers than she could. If at all possible, she had to settle this without lawyers.

She walked through the glass double doors into paradise. Glancing around the remodeled lobby, she took in vaulted ceilings that soared to the roof. Sunshine poured in through huge skylights and fed the potted trees that sat on each side of the two white sofas in the reception area. A polished yellow-wood reception desk sat in the center of everything.

The Montgomerys had been wealthy when she'd been married to Max, and she knew their business had grown. But actually seeing the results of that growth was a staggering reminder of the different stations in the lives of the Montgomerys and the Hunters.

Fear shivered through her. She'd kept wealthy Max Montgomery's daughter away from him for seven years— nearly eight if she counted the pregnancy. Though she'd almost called him a hundred times over the years to tell him about Trisha, to give him a chance to be part of her life, every time she'd picked up the phone she remembered that night. The smashed television. The shattered glasses from the bar shelf. The broken front window. And she'd been afraid. Not just for herself, but for their daughter. He'd made her afraid.

Why should she be the one cowering now, when he'd given her no choice but to leave?

She straightened her shoulders. She would not cower. She would not back down. He'd made this bed. And she would remind him of that. Maybe even ask him if he'd like those details coming out in court if he argued with her over custody or visitation.

Dark brown travertine tile led to the reception desk. The pretty twenty-something redhead manning the station greeted her with a smile. "Can I help you?"

"Yes. I'd like to see Mr. Montgomery."

She glanced down at a small computer screen. "Do you have an appointment?"

"No. But if you'll tell him Kate Hunter Montgomery is here, I'm sure he'll see me."

The young woman glanced over at Kate with raised eyebrows. Kate stood perfectly still under her scrutiny, knowing exactly what the receptionist saw. A small woman with big green eyes and hair just a little bit too thick to tame. Not exactly the woman everyone would expect to be married to a mogul—a ridiculously handsome one at that. With his black hair, blue eyes and tall, lean body, Max had always been a magnet for women. Beautiful women. And he'd chosen her.

It sometimes still puzzled her. Other times it made her realize that having your wishes come true might be the worst thing that could happen.

The receptionist pressed two buttons on her phone, then turned away.

Kate heard only muffled words. Her name. Her description.

Then a wait.

She'd probably called Max's secretary, who had taken the information to Max.

Ten seconds. Twenty seconds. Thirty seconds.

Her face grew warm, her hands clammy. Surely he wasn't so angry that he'd refuse to see her?

Memories of being married to a wealthy man came flooding back. His job was important. His place in the community was even more important. Fundraisers. Ribbon-cuttings. Balls. Parties.

Always worried she'd say or do the wrong thing.

Never feeling good enough.

Righteous indignation surged in her blood. She was the star project manager at her job in Tennessee. She raised a daughter on her own. If she went to a fundraiser, she contributed. If she went to a ribbon-cutting it was for a building she'd helped build.

Good enough?

Hell, yeah. She was good enough. And if Max thought he and his money were going to push her around, he was sadly mistaken.

The receptionist faced her. "I'm sorry, Mrs. Montgomery. You may go up."

"Actually, it's Ms. Hunter now."

The receptionist nodded in acknowledgment. "Take the third elevator in the back of that hall." She pointed to the left. "By the time you get there, a security guard will be there to punch in the code."

She walked to the last elevator with her head high. The security guard said, "Good morning, Ms. Hunter." Proof the receptionist was very good at her job. Punching a few numbers into a keypad, he opened the elevator, motioned her inside and stepped back as the doors closed.

The ride to the fourth floor took seconds. The door swooshed open. More potted trees accented a low, ultra-modern green sofa and chair. A green print rug sat on the yellow hardwood floor.

Sitting at the desk in front of a wall of windows, Max looked up.

Catching him off guard, Kate didn't see the angry father of her child or the rich mogul. She saw Max. Real Max. Max with his thick, unruly black hair. Max with his easy smile and pretty blue eyes. The first time she'd laid eyes on him, he'd stolen her breath and her heart.

Which was another reason she'd moved away rather than simply move out when she'd gotten pregnant. No matter how bad their life, she'd always loved him and he'd always been able to charm her.

She swallowed. Her bravado from the reception area began to fade. But she forced it back to life. She wasn't here to argue for herself, but for Trisha. To protect Trisha.

He rose from his tall-backed, golden-brown leather chair. "Kate. I have to say I'm kind of surprised."

"Yeah. Well, I'm not the wimpy girl you married." There. Best to get that out in the open before they went any further. "We have something to discuss. We're going to discuss it."

"Big talk from a woman who ran away."

"From a drunk," she said, not mincing words. She knew she'd done the right thing and she wasn't going to let his good looks and charm suck her in again. Too much was at stake.

"And hitting below the belt, I see."

"Saying the truth isn't hitting below the belt. Unless you can't handle the truth."

His breath poured out in a long hiss as he motioned toward the green sofa and chair. "I know who and what I am."

She headed for the chair, not wanting to risk that he'd sit beside her on the couch. "Then this conversation should go very easily. We have a daughter. You're sober now. And I'm willing to let you spend time with Trisha as long as I'm with you."

Max lowered himself to the sofa. "With me? I don't get to see my child alone?"

Her chin rose again. "No. Not until I trust you."

Max stared at her. Just as he'd changed over the past eight years, she had, too. Gone was his sweet Kate, replaced by somebody he didn't know. Maybe somebody he didn't want to know. Maybe even somebody who deserved the burst of fury he longed to release.

He rubbed his hands down his face. No matter how much he wanted to rant and rail, he couldn't give in to it. Not only had he been at fault for her leaving, but just as drinking didn't solve anything, neither did losing his temper. Another lesson he'd learned while she was gone.

His voice was perfectly controlled as he said, "I don't think you're in a position to dictate terms."

"I think I am."

"And I have two lawyers who say you aren't."

Her eyes widened with incredulity. "You've already called your lawyers?"

"A smart businessman knows when he needs advice."

"So you think you're going to ride roughshod over me with lawyers?"

"I think I'm going to do what I have to do."

She shook her head. "Do you want me to leave tomorrow? Do you want me to hide so far away and so deeply that you'll never, ever see your daughter?"

Control be damned. "Are you threatening me?"

"I'm protecting my daughter. We play by my rules or no rules at all. I won't put Trisha at risk."

"Risk? You have no reason to fear for her. I never hurt you!"

"No, you just smashed TVs and broke windows. You were escalating, Max, and you scared me."

Guilt pummeled him enough that he scrubbed his hand

over his mouth to give himself a few seconds to collect himself. Finally he said, "You could have talked to me."

Her face scrunched in disbelief. "Really? Talk to a guy so drunk he could barely stand? And how was that supposed to work?"

"I might have come home drunk, but I was sober every morning."

"And hungover."

He sighed. "No matter how I felt, I would have listened to you."

"That's not how I remember it. I remember living with a man who was either stone-cold drunk or hungover. Three years of silence or lies and broken promises. Three years of living with a man who barely noticed I was there. I won't sit back and watch our little girl stare out the window waiting for you the way I used to. Or lie in bed worrying that you'd wrecked your car because you were too drunk to drive and too stubborn to admit it. Or spend the day alone, waiting for you to wake up because you'd been out all night."

Fury rattled through him. "I'm sober now!"

"I see that. And I honestly hope it lasts. But even you can't tell me with absolute certainty that it will. And since you can't, I stand between you and Trisha. I protect her. She will not go through what I went through."

Her voice wobbled, and the anger that had been pulsing through his brain, feeding his replies, stopped dead in its tracks. She wasn't just mad at him. She was still hurting.

She rose and paced to his desk. "Do you know what it's like to live with someone who tells you they love you but then doesn't have ten minutes in a day for you?"

Max went stock-still. This was usually what happened when he apologized. The person he'd wronged had a grievance. It had been so long since he'd had one of these sessions that he'd forgotten. But when Kate turned, her green eyes wary, her voice soft, filled with repressed pain, remorse flooded him. She had a right to be angry.

"I'll tell you what it's like. It's painful, but most of all it's bone-shatteringly lonely."

Guilt tightened his stomach. He'd always known he'd hurt her, but he'd never been sober enough to hear the pain in her voice, see it shimmer in her eyes.

And she wanted to save Trisha from that. So did he. But the way he'd protect her would be to stay sober. "I won't hurt her."

"You know, you always told me the same thing. That you wouldn't hurt me. But you did. Every day." Her voice softened to a faint whisper. "Every damned day."

He squeezed his eyes shut. "I'm sorry. Really sorry."

"Right."

Righteous indignation rose up in him. He hated his past as much as she hated his past. But this time she wasn't innocent.

"Did you ever stop to think that maybe I'd have gotten sober sooner if I'd known I was having a child? Did you ever stop to think that if you'd stayed, I might have turned around an entire year sooner?"

"No." She caught his gaze. "You loved me, Max. I always knew it. But I wasn't a good enough reason for you to get sober. I wasn't taking a chance with our child."

"You could have at least told me you were pregnant before you left."

"And have you show up drunk at the hospital while I was struggling through labor? Or drunk on Christmas Day to ruin Trisha's first holiday? Or maybe have you stagger into her dance recital so she could be embarrassed in front of her friends?" She shook her head. "I don't think so."

The picture she painted shamed him. Things he'd done drunk now embarrassed him as much as they had his friends and family. And he suddenly understood. Making amends with Kate wouldn't be as simple as saying he was sorry. He was going to have to prove himself to her.

He blew his breath out on a sigh, accepted it, because accepting who he was, who he had been, was part of his recovery. "So maybe it would be good for you to be around when I see her."

Her reply was soft, solemn. "Maybe it would."

"Can I come over tonight and meet her?"

"I was thinking tomorrow afternoon might be a better idea. I take my mom to the hospital every day, but lately Trisha's been bored. So I thought I'd start bringing her home in the afternoon."

"And I can come over?"

"Yes. Until my dad is released from the hospital, we'll have some privacy."

With that she turned and headed for the elevator. Prickling with guilt, he leaned back on the sofa. But when the elevator doors swished closed behind her, he thought about how different things might have been if she'd told him about her pregnancy, and his anger returned. She hadn't given him a chance to try to sober up. She hadn't even given him a chance to be a dad.

Still, could he blame her?

A tiny voice deep down inside him said yes. He could blame her. He might see her perspective, but he'd also had a right to know his child.

He rose from the sofa and headed for his desk again. That's exactly what his father had told him the night he'd confronted him about being his adopted brother Chance's biological father. About bringing his illegitimate son into their home with a lie. A sham. An adoption used to cover an affair.

I had a right to know my child.

He ran his hand across his forehead as nerves and more anger surged through him. He hadn't thought about that part of his life in years. His brother had run away the night Max had confronted their dad. Which was part of why Max drank. At AA he'd learned to put those troubles behind him, but now, suddenly, here he was again, wondering. Missing his brother with a great ache that gnawed at his belly. Because Kate was home and Kate was part of that time in his life.

Losing Chance might have been the event that pushed him over the edge with his alcoholism, but he wasn't that guy anymore. He hadn't been for seven long years. He only hoped seeing Kate, fighting with Kate, meeting a daughter he hadn't known he had, didn't tempt that guy out of hiding.

He grabbed his cell phone from his desk and hit the speed-dial number for his sponsor.

CHAPTER TWO

THE FOLLOWING AFTERNOON, Max left the office at noon and raced home to put on jeans and a T-shirt. Something more comfortable, more casual, than a black suit and white shirt, so he didn't intimidate his daughter. Or Kate.

Like it or not, he had things to make up to her. His sponsor, Joe Zubek, had reminded him of that. He had to take responsibility for everything he'd done while drunk, and he'd hurt Kate—mistreated her enough that she didn't want their daughter to suffer the same fate.

He had to take responsibility.

He chose the Range Rover over the Mercedes and drove past the expensive houses and estates in the lush part of the city in which he lived. Once off the hill, he headed across the bridge, through Pine Ward's business district to the blue-collar section of town where little Cape Cods mixed and mingled with older two-story homes and a few newer ranch houses.

He made three turns to get to Elm Street and there it was. The redbrick, two-story house he'd loved. Not just because Kate had lived there, but because it had a wide front porch and a swing.

He stopped his vehicle and simply stared at the porch, the swing. He couldn't count the number of times he and Kate had made out on that swing.

His eyes drifted shut at the memory. She'd been eighteen to his twenty-four. Not necessarily a huge age difference but Kate had been sheltered. So he'd had to go slow with her, be cautious. But when they'd finally made love—in a room sprinkled with rose petals and filled with soft candlelight— oh, Lord. He'd known—he'd absolutely known—she was the only woman in the world for him. They were together for nine years. Four years of dating until she graduated university, and five years of marriage. When she'd left him, he'd missed her so much he sometimes thought his heart would wither and die.

And now she was back.

He popped open his eyes and yanked the key from the Rover's ignition. It didn't matter. He'd screwed up their relationship permanently and there was no going back. Besides, his current time with Kate wouldn't be about them. It would be about their daughter. And he wouldn't lose the chance to know Trisha by foolishly wanting to rekindle a romance that was dead. He'd killed it. He had to remember that.

He strode up the sidewalk and across the plank porch without as much as a glance in the direction of the swing.

When he rang the bell, Kate instantly opened the door, as if she'd been waiting for him. Wearing a short white shirt that didn't quite reach her low-riding jeans, with bare feet and toenails painted a bright blue, she looked closer to twenty than thirty-five. Her thick dark hair swirled around her.

His racing heart stuttered. She wasn't what anyone would call conventionally beautiful, but she had an innate sexuality that stopped most men in their tracks. Including him. After his thoughts in the car, thoughts of making out on a porch swing and making love to her in a hotel room filled with candles, he couldn't keep his gaze from taking a second trip down her trim body to her sexy toes and back up again.

He had to swallow before he could say, "Hey."

"Come in, Max."

He stepped inside the simple foyer. Pale beige floor tiles led to hardwood floors in both the dining room on the right and the living room on the left.

She motioned to the peach-and-beige sofa and matching chairs—the same furniture that had been in the room when they were married. "Let's sit."

As he turned to go into the living room, he caught a glimpse of Trisha peeking out of the kitchen. She smiled shyly at him. His heart began to thrum in his chest. She had Kate's pretty pixie face, his blue eyes. She was an adorable little image of both of them.

Kate also saw Trisha and she laughed. "Come on, sweetie. Don't be shy. Come into the living room with Mommy." Then she walked to the sofa, motioning for him to sit on one of the two club chairs across from her.

Trisha entered slowly, shyly, sidling up beside the arm of the sofa where her mom sat, as Max lowered himself to a club chair.

Kate didn't waste any time. "Trisha, this is the man I told you about." She paused just for a second. "Your father."

Trisha glanced at the floor. "Hi."

"Hi." He'd never felt so much so fast. Fear and wonder filled him simultaneously, along with a fresh burst of anger. He was clumsy right now, tongued-tied with his own child because Kate had kept her from him. "I…um…it's nice to meet you."

Trish nodded.

Kate said, "Trisha will be starting second grade in the fall."

"Second grade," Max repeated, his tongue thick, his brain a ball of melting wax. Thoughts beeped in his head like neon signs. Had Kate stayed, he'd know his little girl. He might have seen her birth. He might have gotten sober sooner—

They might still be married.

He sucked in a breath. Told himself to stop those thoughts.

All of them. He had to take responsibility. "That's...I remember having fun in second grade."

She peeked up at him. "I had fun in first grade."

"Trisha's a very good student. Her teachers love her."

Trisha smiled again, this time revealing two missing front teeth.

His heart skipped a beat. A laugh bubbled to his chest. She was so damned cute.

"Teachers always like the kids who get good grades."

Kate's mom entered the room carrying a tray, surprising Max. He'd thought they were supposed to be alone.... Then he understood. Kate didn't trust him enough to be alone with him.

Bev smiled brightly. Too brightly. "I have lemonade and cookies if anybody's interested."

Trish reached for a cookie even before Bev had the tray on the table.

Kate laughed. "Where are your manners? Your dad's a guest in our house. We offer him a cookie first."

Trisha reluctantly brought her hand back and caught his gaze. "Do you want a cookie?"

Max's chest tightened. He had a daughter he didn't know, a little girl who, right now, was probably as uncomfortable with him as he was with her, and a shivering ex-mother-in-law, trying to pretend everything was okay. All because Kate had kept them apart. And why? Because she was afraid? He'd never physically hurt her. Never.

He struggled with the urge to shout an obscenity and then struggled not to squeeze his eyes shut in frustration. He couldn't think like this. He wasn't allowed. He had to take responsibility for his actions. He couldn't blame someone else.

He forced a smile for Trisha. "Sure. Yeah. I'd love a cookie."

Bev offered the plate to him. He took one of the fat chocolate chip cookies. Nobody spoke.

After a few bites, Trisha broke the silence. "Do you like the cookie?"

This time his smile wasn't forced. When he looked at her sweet face, he just wanted to hug her. He longed to put his arms around her and feel his own child in his arms.

"Yes. I like the cookie very much." He cleared his throat, reminded himself to stay in the moment. If he was here for Trisha, he would be here for Trisha. Really here. "So what about your friends? Do you have lots of friends?"

"Sunny and Jeffrey."

His gaze shot to Kate's. "Her best friends are boys?"

Trisha giggled. The sound skipped along his nerve endings, warming his heart, filling him with awe. This was his daughter. His baby girl. If he wanted to be in her life, he couldn't dwell in the past. He had to live in today. This minute.

"Sunny's a girl."

"Oh, I was thinking Sonny."

She frowned.

He smiled. "Never mind. What's your favorite game? Do you play T-ball? Little League?"

Confused by his question, Trisha glanced at her mom who said, "Those are sports."

She faced him again with a big toothless grin. "No."

Kate rose. "Do we want to do something?"

He glanced up at her.

She motioned with her hand. "So we have something to do other than trying to think of something to say."

He looked at Trisha. "What would you like to do?"

She glanced down shyly. Kate stooped in front of her. "Why don't you take your dad to the family room and have a tea party?"

Excitement filled her eyes. She nodded and led him down the hall, into a family room that was neat as a pin except for toys littering the brown tweed sofa and chair. A red plastic child-sized table sat in the center of the room. Dolls and stuffed animals sat on the yellow, blue and green chairs surrounding it.

Trisha plucked the toys from their seats and tossed them to the sofa before she pointed at one of the chairs. "You sit here."

He peered down at the little plastic chair.

But before he could say anything, Kate said, "Maybe Daddy's too big for a chair?"

That blasted, unwanted anger surged in Max again. "You don't need to answer for me. You've made enough of my decisions to last a lifetime."

Kate faced him, eyebrows arched as if asking if he really wanted to get into that fight now, and he immediately regretted saying anything. Especially in front of Trisha.

He backpedaled. "It's just that the chair looks sturdy enough." And he could also keep his weight shifted in such a way he wouldn't put too much stress on it. He smiled at Trisha. "It's fine." And back at Kate. "I'll be fine."

Carefully, he lowered himself to the colorful chair and sighed gratefully when it held his weight. Though his knees were taller than the table and he felt like a giant, he was seated.

Trisha held out her teapot to her mom. "Can we have some tea?"

Kate took the pot. "Sure. I'll get you some more cookies too."

While she was gone, Trisha kept her attention on arranging little cups and saucers. "This is my snack."

"Your snack?"

She almost looked at him. "My afternoon snack."

"Oh." He got it now. "So you're not getting extra cookies."

She glanced up. Actually looked at him this time. "Too much sugar isn't good for me."

He laughed, recognizing she'd probably repeated verbatim what she'd been told by her mom.

He made himself a little more comfortable on the chair. Trisha finally sat. Thirty seconds went by with neither of them saying a word. Panic filled him, along with the fear of total inadequacy. How did a man parent a child he was only now meeting?

Kate walked into the room carrying the teapot and a small plate with three cookies. She'd tucked her dark hair behind her ears, revealing the slim column of her throat. His gaze fell from her throat to her T-shirt, which perfectly outlined her breasts, to the trim line of her tummy exposed above the waistband of her jeans. His breath stuttered. His attraction to her sprang up like a lion that had been lying in wait in the African bush, confusing him. How could he be so damned attracted to a woman he was so damned angry with?

"One cookie for you. Two for your dad."

Trisha sighed. "Because he's bigger."

"Exactly."

She offered the plate of cookies to him, standing close enough that he could smell her cologne.

Telling himself he'd better get accustomed to being around her or he'd drive himself crazy, he took a cookie from the tray. "No cookie for you?"

She walked away and began gathering the toys from the sofa. "Not hungry. Besides, this isn't my party. It's yours. With your daughter. Enjoy it."

Panic swamped him again. Unwanted attraction be damned. He needed Kate and she was deserting him.

Trisha poured the "tea." Wary of the cleanliness of the plastic cup and whatever was inside, he cast Kate a questioning look. "Am I allowed to ask when these little cups were last washed?"

She laughed lightly. "We wash the tea set every time she uses it. It's clean."

Still cautious, he took a sip and discovered the drink was actually a grape punch of some sort. Dark enough to look like tea, but not really tea. "It's good."

"It's the queen's favorite."

He glanced at Trisha. "The queen?"

Trisha pointed to an empty chair. "The queen comes to everyone's tea parties."

So out of his element he had no clue what to say or do, he again looked to Kate. But she was busy gathering toys. Either not paying attention or deliberately forcing him to figure out something to say. With her arms full, he expected her to walk to a toy box, but there was no box. Instead, she stacked the toys in an empty corner.

It suddenly occurred to him that she lived somewhere else. Somewhere so far away they'd never even accidentally bumped into each other. And she didn't visit. So how did Trisha have toys here?

He knocked on the plastic table. "Are these new?"

Kate said, "Bought them our second day here. Trisha and I both needed a distraction."

Remembering her dad's stroke, sorrow unexpectedly swamped him. "I...um...I really am sorry about your dad."

"He'll be fine, but no one's sure how long he'll be in the hospital." She reached for another toy. "So I took a three-month leave of absence so we can be here for Mom. That's a long time to be away from home, and a little girl's gotta be entertained, so we bought some stuff."

He blinked, taking all that in. "You'll be here three months?"

She picked up another toy. "Yep."

They'd be here three months. He had time. Blessed, blessed

time. But he also understood why Kate believed Trisha would need to be entertained. And maybe that could be his avenue to getting visits alone with her. If he could take her while Kate was busy with her father, he could be a savior of sorts, not an interruption.

"You know, if there's ever a time when you can't take her with you to the hospital or whatever, I'd be happy to clear my schedule and babysit."

She peered at him. "Thanks. But we already agreed that I'd be with you when you visited Trisha."

He should have known that wouldn't work. But that didn't mean he couldn't do something to prove he would be there for them. "Is there anything else she needs?"

Kate turned. "She's right there in front of you. Ask her."

Annoyance skittered through him. He was trying to be nice and she was snippy? If he was inept in this situation, it was her fault. But he kept his cool, reminded himself that he had to take the blame for Kate's distrust and be patient. No matter how unfair it seemed to him, he still had to play by her rules.

He faced Trisha. "Is there anything you need?"

"A pony."

Kate laughed. He shot her a look, but turned back to Trisha. Though he was brand-new at being a daddy, he wasn't a stranger to dealing with people, negotiating, pointing out the obvious. Until he knew how to be a daddy, he'd simply use the skills he had. "There's no barn here for a pony."

"That's what my mom says."

"So is there anything you need aside from a pony?" A thought hit him and he quickly added, "Or an elephant or a snake or any other living thing."

She giggled. "I don't want an elephant."

Thinking back to his brother Chance, he picked up his cup to sip again and said, "Some kids do."

* * *

Kate had to stifle a spontaneous laugh, but just as quickly guilt pummeled her. He wouldn't be feeling his way around parenting right now if she hadn't left.

But he was doing okay, and the more he visited, the better he'd be. Her staying here three months would give him plenty of time to learn how to be a daddy. Especially if he visited a few times a week.

She almost groaned. Good God. A few times a week? If she insisted on being part of every visit—and she already had—she was about to spend the better part of three months with her ex-husband.

Trisha began to pretend to feed her bear. Max glanced back at Kate, then rose from his little plastic chair and walked over to her.

"I'm not sure what the protocol is here, but I don't want to overstay my welcome."

Though it killed her, she politely said, "You're fine. We don't have to be at the hospital until seven."

"I know, but it's just that we had a nice visit and I don't want to spoil it by boring her."

Familiar fear spiraled through her. "You're ditching her?"

"Not ditching. Keeping her from disliking me because I bore her."

She fought the instinctive anger that rose in her—remnants of the insult of always being left alone while he drank with his friends—and forced herself to be logical, not emotional. Their visit had been good, albeit short. Nice, short visits would get Trisha accustomed to him. And get him accustomed to Trisha without pushing either one of them.

"Okay." Eager to get away from him, she walked over to the table and tapped on it to get Trisha's attention. "Your dad is leaving now." She picked up the teapot. "Say goodbye."

Trisha gave him her toothless grin. "Bye."

As goodbyes went, that left a lot to be desired. Seeing the

confused look on Max's face, Kate sucked in a breath and did what she had to do. "Give your dad a hug."

Trisha got up from her chair and went to her father. She wrapped her arms around his legs, squeezed quickly and pulled back. "Bye."

He closed his eyes, savoring the hug, then stooped down beside her and took her into his arms. Guilt tightened Kate's stomach, but realism knocked it out of position. He might be a nice guy now—might—she suspected all this good behavior could be an act—but he'd ruined their marriage with his drinking. He'd forced her away. And she'd take Trisha away from him again in a heartbeat if he started drinking.

"Bye." He rose and left. Quickly and quietly.

Relieved that he was gone, Kate carried the dishes out to the kitchen where her mom was wiping down a countertop. Trisha skipped in after her.

Sliding onto a chair by the table she said, "I liked him."

Kate and her mom exchanged a glance, and Bev said, "Yeah. He's a peach."

Trisha giggled. "He's not a peach. Peaches are fruit." She grabbed an apple from the bowl on the table and skipped out of the room.

Kate's mom rounded on her. "So?"

"So, what?"

"So do you think you appeased him? Is he going to do something like file for custody?"

Kate slumped against the sink. "With Trisha around, we didn't really have time to talk about anything."

"Oh, Katie! That was the whole point of the visit. Making him happy enough that he didn't go to court." She sighed and turned back to the sink. "I think you're going to have to go talk to him."

Even the thought made her stomach jump. She didn't want to see him. But if she didn't pin him down, he could easily pick up a phone, an entire staff of lawyers would be drafting motions and she could potentially lose control. At least this way, she called the shots. She would say when Trisha saw him. And she also would stay with them while he visited.

Slim as it was, she had an upper hand and she had to keep it.

CHAPTER THREE

MAX LEFT THE HOUSE with tears in his eyes. His first hug from his daughter had been quick, almost an afterthought. One of the biggest moments of his life had been treated as an afterthought.

He sucked in a breath, forcing himself to face some realities. Though it was momentous for him, it might have actually been scary for a little girl to hug a man who was a virtual stranger. So he couldn't be angry that Kate had seemed flip about asking Trisha to hug him. She might have done it for Trisha's sake. He had to take it in stride.

But so many things whirled around in his head. Anger with himself for ruining his marriage, his entire life for so many years. The desire to be angry with Kate. The argument that he couldn't be angry with Kate. The sure knowledge that he had to take responsibility. His head was so full of thoughts and his heart so full of emotion that he wasn't even sure if he was right or wrong.

Walking to the Range Rover, he grabbed his cell phone and hit speed dial.

His personal secretary answered. "Hey, boss."

"I'm not coming back this afternoon."

Silence. Annette was the only person who knew where he'd been—knew about Trisha.

"Is everything okay?"

"Peachy."

"It doesn't sound peachy."

Forty-five, with four kids of varying ages, Annette was wise beyond her years. She was also someone he trusted.

"I need to think some of this through."

"The talk with your wife didn't go so well?"

Talk? They'd barely spoken, and when they had, an argument had always huddled just below the surface. He drew in a breath. "We didn't shout."

"Well, that's a start."

He laughed.

"Look, it's Friday afternoon anyway. You haven't had a day off in probably a decade. I'll hold down the fort."

He opened the door of the Range Rover. "Why don't you go home, too?"

"Hey, you don't have to ask me twice."

With that she clicked off and Max drove home. He walked into his silent foyer and stopped as memories flooded him. When he and Kate were first married, she would greet him at the door. Sometimes naked. He shook his head. They had been so in love it was hard to fathom that they could barely hold a conversation now.

Walking toward the kitchen, he was grateful that his housekeeper was gone for the day. With his mom in Houston visiting friends, he didn't have to worry about interruptions or having to make small talk—or having to tell her she had a granddaughter she didn't know about.

He winced. That conversation was not going to be pretty. His mom would either explode with anger or melt into a puddle of emotion. And he'd have to remind her that Kate had had good reason to leave. Just as if it were eight years ago, he was back to facing the consequences of his drinking.

He walked to the master bedroom. It was the one room he had changed after he'd sobered up. He couldn't handle the memories. Not just making love, but the arguments. Arguments he'd caused. If he closed his eyes, he could still hear Kate begging him to stop drinking, hear his own arrogant proclamations that he was fine. What an idiot he'd been.

He quickly changed into swimming trunks and made his way to the pool. He dived in with a resounding splash and surfaced, spraying water everywhere when he shook his head from side to side.

"Hey."

Kate's voice surprised him and his heart jumped. He spun around. "Hey."

She took a few steps closer to the pool. "I… We never talked about visitation. About when you'd see her again." She paused, smiled weakly. "When I called your office, Annette told me you'd gone home." Her smile became genuine. "It's nice that she still works for you."

He cautiously headed for the ladder. Seeing Kate by the pool brought another cascade of memories. Mostly because she hadn't changed physically; she looked the same. She sounded the same. It was as if she hadn't ever gone away. As if he still had the right to take her in his arms and kiss her.

His heart pitter-pattered. Not because she'd probably deck him if he tried, but from an unexpected burst of longing. He hadn't ever really gotten over her, just told himself to forget her because he'd driven her away. Now that she was back, he had an entire marriage full of memories and emotions surfacing, confusing him.

"Visitation?"

"More like planning your next time with Trisha."

He took a step toward her.

She took a step back. "Tomorrow's Saturday, I thought you might have time to see her again."

"I'll make time."

She smiled tentatively. "That's great."

He could see her in the green bikini. Remember the sun shimmering off her hair. Remember her giggle.

"Is one o'clock too early tomorrow?"

"No. I'll drive Mom to the hospital around noon. Trish and I will be back by one."

He nodded.

She gestured vaguely toward the driveway. "Guess I'll go."

Don't let her go!

Yearning surged up in him. Not for a kiss or sex or even a chance to flirt. Just the opportunity to be with her. To see how she'd been. See who she was now that eight years had gone by. Just to be in her company again. "Or you could stay and we could talk about some things."

She shielded her eyes from the sun. "We do have some things to resolve."

"Like child support. I haven't paid a cent in eight years. I'm guessing I owe you a bundle."

"I think I forfeited that when I left."

"I don't."

"Don't worry about it."

"I'm not worried. I just…I just…" He combed his fingers through his hair. "I want to know things about Trisha." *And hear the sound of your voice while you talk.* "Things like her favorite foods. Her favorite teacher. What she doesn't like." *And hear the lilt in your voice when you talk about her.*

"She's a normal little girl. There's not much to say."

He directed her to the French doors that led to the family room. "You can tell me about her first tooth. Her first words."

Guilt tightened Kate's stomach again. Without being accusatory, he'd reminded her that he'd missed some important milestones in their child's life.

Could she blame him for wanting to know?

Could she deny him?

No. Not only was telling him about their daughter fair, but

it might also ease some of the tension of the next day's visit and maybe even prevent him from running to his lawyers. She didn't want to make friends with him, but she did have to deal with him. A good conversation might go a long way to fixing their awkwardness. "Sure."

He opened the door and motioned for her to enter first. When she saw the family room was the same as she'd decorated it, a symphony of butterflies took flight in her stomach. He might not have wanted to do the work required to change the green granite fireplace and hardwood floors. But why keep a sofa and chairs that could have been replaced long ago? Why keep her knickknacks? The art she'd chosen?

He walked toward the kitchen of the open-floor-plan downstairs. "Iced tea?"

"Yes. Thanks." She'd need something to swallow the lump of emotion clogging her throat. She remembered the first time they'd stepped into this house, when it was little more than framework and plywood. They'd bought it new, not yet complete, so they could put their stamp on it.

She brushed her hand along a white wood chair rail, lovingly caressed the drum shade of a lamp.

He handed her a glass of iced tea.

"Thanks." She looked up, caught his gaze, and her stomach plummeted to the floor. It was like thirteen years ago, when he was young and sweet and not pressured by the business or his family. Her chest tingled. Her already weak knees liquefied.

Oh, surely she wasn't going to let herself be attracted to him?

He motioned for her to sit on the chair and he sat on the sofa in his wet trunks. "So start with her birthday." He grimaced. "I guess I'd like to know what day she was born. Were there any complications?" He caught her gaze. "Were you okay?"

The concern in his voice brought back her feeling of connection to him, the younger him, the guy who'd loved her. She swallowed, fighting it. "I was fine. It was a normal pregnancy." She smiled wistfully. "She was born on July 27 after about eighteen hours of labor."

He sat back. "Ouch."

She batted a hand. "It was normal. Nothing every other woman in the world doesn't go through." A thought struck her. "I have pictures."

He sat up. "You do?"

"What mother doesn't?"

With a laugh, she flipped through her wallet to find the pictures she carried of Trisha. Luckily, she was packrat enough to have kept every special-event picture she had, even the infant photo from the hospital.

Sitting beside him on the sofa, she presented the wallet displaying the pictures. "Here's her first picture."

He laughed. "She looks like a prune."

"That's from floating around in amniotic fluid for nine months." She flipped to the next picture, the one taken at a studio when Trisha was three months old. "This one's better."

He sighed an "Ah," and said, "She was adorable."

Hearing the emotion in his voice, she slid the picture from its wallet slot. "You can have this one."

His gaze shot to hers. "I can?"

She quickly looked away. "Sure. I have lots of photos that I can send you."

"I—" He swallowed. "Thanks."

She felt the weird vibe again. She'd hated this man, feared him for so long that she'd kept his child from him. And now here they were sitting together, talking like normal people, when inside he probably disliked her as much for keeping Trisha from him as she disliked him for ruining their marriage.

She handed him her wallet and rose from the sofa, getting away from him. "The next six or eight pictures are Trisha. Just go ahead and flip through."

He did as she asked, pausing over every picture in the wallet, intensifying her guilt. Especially since she was standing in the house where she'd loved him. Where they'd been so happy.

But a quick glance at the window sliced through all her good memories and brought her back to reality. He'd broken that window the night she'd left. She hadn't been wrong to run. She might have been able to stay if she'd only had herself to think about. But she'd had a baby. An unborn bundle of joy. And he had been escalating. His behavior got worse every day. She'd done the right thing.

After a minute, he handed the wallet back to her. "Those are—" He sucked in a breath. "I can't even describe what I feel."

She brusquely took the wallet. Shoved it into her purse. Ready to head for the door, she said, "I'll send you my extra photos. I'll make sure I get one from every stage of her life so far."

Before she could even turn to make her escape, he said, "How about her teeth? I notice two of them are missing."

She hesitated. The door beckoned. But in the end, she turned around. She owed him at least one conversation to catch him up on what he'd missed.

"She lost those last month. Together." She gingerly sat on the chair again. "It scared her to death, but when the tooth fairy put a twenty-dollar bill under her pillow she got over it."

He chuckled. The deep, rich sound brought back a happy memory of him lifting her off her feet and twirling her around as he laughed. Sadness rattled through her. She hadn't thought of that in eight years.

She hadn't thought any good thing about him in eight years—probably longer. All the memories of their love had been blackened by memories of his drinking. In a sense, their good times had been stolen from her. But here in this house, with sober Max, they were coming back to her. And, oh, how she'd missed those.

She glanced around again, her heart in her throat. Remembering those wonderful things from the beginning of their marriage might be risky, but she didn't care. Just for ten minutes, she wanted to be reminded that she hadn't been an idiot who'd fallen for a drunk, but a normal girl who'd fallen for a wonderful guy.

"The tooth fairy, huh?"

Knocked out of her reverie, she faced him again. "Yeah. I'm pretty sure she knows it's me who leaves the money, but she's okay with it."

"I guess she no longer believes in Santa Claus, the Easter Bunny, that kind of stuff."

"No. You missed those."

She'd meant that to sound flippant and fun. Instead, when the words left her mouth the room became silent.

And stayed silent so long that she couldn't take it anymore. The big elephant in the room was that he might have been a drunk, but she'd hidden his child from him. She'd had good reason. Tons of good reasons. But could a woman really keep a child from her father without at least a little remorse? A sense of responsibility for hurting him, no matter how bad a husband he'd been?

"I'm sorry."

He glanced up sharply, caught her gaze. "For what?"

"For hurting you by keeping Trisha from you."

"You did what you had to do."

Relief saturated her. "You accept that?"

"I have to."

"Part of twelve steps?"

"In a roundabout way."

He was so calm. So accepting. So different.

Confused, she scooped her glass of iced tea from the coffee table. He genuinely seemed committed. And that could be nothing but good for Trisha. But it also intensified her guilt.

"So," he said, obviously changing the subject. "I noticed she had a lot of dolls."

"Most little girls do."

"Going to be weird for me to insinuate myself into her life."

Since he was trying and she was tired of feeling guilty, maybe she should just do what he was doing—pretend nothing was wrong? "I'll help you."

"That'd be great."

He smiled a genuine smile and her heart swelled with longing as her brain filled with memories of him before he'd started drinking, when he was young, happy, downright silly sometimes.

The conversation died again. She glanced around at the room she'd decorated and looked beyond it to her kitchen, her living room. Even the foyer tables, lamps and art that were her choices.

He'd loved her. He'd loved her enough to give her a free hand and then enjoy what she'd chosen. They'd been so happy—

Tears blurred her eyes and she bounced out of her seat. "You know what? I've gotta go."

He rose. "Okay."

She raced toward the French doors. Damn him for being so accommodating! So nice. So easygoing now. Now, when it didn't matter. Now, when there was no going back.

The sense of loss swelled in her. Halfway to the doors, she spun around. "You ruined it."

He didn't even attempt to pretend he didn't know what she was talking about. "I know."

"We had it all! Everything other couples longed for. Money. A house. A great sex life. Laughter. And you threw it all away!"

"Why do you think I quit drinking? Because I know that! At first when you left, I was so lonely and miserable that I drank more. Then one day it hit me that I'd done this to my-self—" He blew his breath out on a sigh. "I'd done this to us. And that's when I went to AA."

The last thing she wanted to hear was that he'd quit drinking because he knew that was why he'd lost her. It hurt too much. The tears on her eyelids threatened to spill over and she tightened her jaw.

"I also know I've had seven years to get past a lot of stuff that you're just facing now."

His voice was soft, apologetic. But that only made it worse. Her tears teetered on the edges of her eyelids, then tumbled onto her cheeks.

She pivoted and raced to the door. She had to get the hell out of here.

"Kate, don't."

She stopped, her hand on the doorknob. "Don't what? Don't leave? Don't care?"

"It doesn't do any good to put yourself through the mess of remembering everything every time you see me. It's over. It's done. We might have lost us, but we have a daughter. And that's something wonderful for me. So don't go back in time wishing for what could have been. Just help me deal with today."

Her chin wobbled with the effort not to sob. He'd had so much time to get over this that it almost seemed as if he had no emotion about their lost marriage.

But she did.

And it hurt.

Damn it. It hurt.

Tears streaming down her cheeks, she yanked open the door. "Sure. Fine. You can come by again tomorrow at one."

CHAPTER FOUR

SATURDAY MAX ARRIVED at the Hunter residence with a gift. A small doll. He'd called Annette and she'd told him little girls usually liked fashion dolls that they could dress up. So he'd gone to a toy store and purchased one, along with several outfits.

He wasn't trying to buy Trisha's affection, but he did think the doll would give them something to talk about.

He rang the front-door bell and waited, tensing, for what he wasn't sure. Things hadn't gone so well with Kate the day before. He could see her struggle. How fair was it that one day he decided never to drink again, asked for forgiveness and just moved on? It didn't help that he was sorry. Sorry didn't take away the pain. Or fix the memories. All he could offer her was the advice to move on.

From the alcoholic who'd hurt her, it was probably small comfort.

Realizing a few minutes had gone by, he rang the bell again. No one came. He frowned and walked to the edge of the porch. Leaning around, he saw no car in the driveway. She'd said she had to take her mom to the hospital at noon. Maybe she'd gotten hung up?

He didn't even have her cell phone number to call her. And after the way she'd left the day before, he didn't really feel comfortable asking for it.

So many things to work out. And none of it was going to be easy. But because they had a child, she was forced back into his life. Now she was struggling to forgive him and he was struggling with a pointless attraction.

He glanced around again, accepting that she wasn't home and not sure what to do. Finally, he lowered himself to the swing. With one foot, he set it in motion. The temptation was strong to close his eyes and remember...

Kissing her soft sweet lips.

Longing for her to say the right words on hot summer nights when she was home for school vacation so he could seduce her—

But he didn't. He didn't seduce her on any one of those nights on the swing and he didn't let his mind drift too far today. It was better to deal with the present rather than escaping into the past. Especially since he knew how that past had turned out.

The sound of a car coming down the street opened his eyes and he glanced up just as it pulled into the driveway.

He rose. Before he got to the side of the porch, car doors began to open. Kate levered herself out of the driver's side as Trisha bounced out of the back seat right behind her.

She raced to the other side of the car. "I'll help Grandpa."

Kate ran after her. "No! I'll help Grandpa." She glanced at her mom as she got out of the passenger's side front seat. "Mom, give Trisha the house key so she can open the kitchen door."

As Bev rifled through her purse for a key, Max headed for the porch steps. In a few strides he was at the driveway, near the car's back door where Kate and her mom hovered. "Can I help?"

Bev said, "Yes!" as Kate faced him and solemnly said, "We've got it."

"I'm not sure we do," Bev said, obviously not comfortable taking her ex-son-in-law's side over her daughter's, but equally uncomfortable dealing with her sick husband. "I'd appreciate someone stronger than I am helping us get him up the steps."

"I'm glad to help."

Bev opened the back door of the car as Trisha yelled, "Kitchen door's open," from the side porch.

Kate walked to the trunk of the car and unloaded several bags and a suitcase.

But when Max reached inside to help Kate's dad, Dennis Hunter shrugged away from his hold. "I'm fine. I can do this myself."

Kate raced over with a walker. "Here, Dad. Try this."

He grunted and grumbled as he got out of the car and once again shrugged away from Max's hand when he tried to assist him, though he let Kate wrap her fingers around his biceps.

Dennis shakily leaned against the walker, but by that time Max had figured out his help wouldn't be accepted. So, grabbing the bags and the suitcase, he walked ahead of them, making sure there was nothing in the way as Dennis hobbled to the back-porch steps. With Kate's assistance, Dennis gingerly climbed them. Max stood off to the left, just in case.

"He's a stubborn man," Bev said, coming up beside him.

"And he's probably not too fond of me."

Bev shook her head. "No. He's not. But right now, this is all about his pride."

When Kate had her dad in the house, Max and Bev walked up to the porch. He appreciated Bev's candor, if only because honesty made it possible for him to know what to do. If she wasn't telling him to leave, he knew it was okay to stay.

As they entered through the kitchen door, Max saw Kate and her dad hobbling toward the front foyer. He and Bev followed them.

"Just set those things on the floor in front of the living

room. This morning we turned it into a makeshift bedroom for him," Bev said, as she and Max followed Kate and Dennis down the hall. By the time they got to the doorway, Kate had her dad seated on what looked to be a hospital bed.

Bev brazened her way into the room. "Come on, you old coot. Stop your snipping. The doctor said you needed to be careful for the first few weeks. We're just helping you to be careful."

Dennis growled something Max couldn't make out. From the corner of his eye, he saw Trisha sitting on the steps. His daughter smiled shyly at him. Knowing he wasn't wanted— or maybe even needed—by Dennis or Kate in the makeshift bedroom, he sat on the step below Trisha. "How's it going?"

She shrugged.

"I brought you a present."

Her face lit up. "You did?"

"Yeah, I left it on the swing. Let me go get it."

He walked out to the front porch and grabbed the bag containing the fashion-model doll. But when he entered the foyer, there was so much commotion going on with Dennis wanting the TV on, then wanting it off again, that Max nudged his head in the direction of the family room. "Why don't we go in the family room?"

Trisha nodded and scrambled down the steps, leading the way.

She ran toward her little table, but he suggested they sit on the sofa. "Just until we get the present out of the bag."

She nodded eagerly and raced to the sofa. He eased himself down beside her. Painfully honest, he said, "I asked my secretary for suggestions. And she told me you would like this."

He handed her the bag and she all but dove inside. "Rachel!" she cried, giving the popular doll's name.

He smiled. "You like it?"

"Yes!" Then she rose up on her knees and propelled herself at him.

Max's heart stopped. She was soft and warm and innocently sincere. How easily she seemed to be getting adjusted to him. Now if he could only adjust as easily to her.

She slid off the sofa and ran to her little table and chairs. "She has to come to a tea party."

Max stayed on the sofa but quickly realized he would be totally out of everything if he stayed there. So he rose and made his way to the little table.

Without looking at him, she said, "Since Mom's busy, we'll just have pretend tea."

She ripped the packaging away from her new doll, and he lowered himself to a chair. "Sounds good to me."

"She said Grandpa would be sick for a while." She peeked up at him, her little face drawn in sad lines. "I don't want him to be sick."

"He's not really sick anymore. More like recovering."

Her face brightened. "Not sick?"

Ugh. Maybe he shouldn't have said anything? But now that he was in, he was in and he had to keep going. "He was sick. Very sick. And because he was very sick, certain parts of him don't work as well as they used to."

Her eyes widened in horror.

His chest tightened with fear. Had he made things worse? Good Lord, he was terrible at this. Which meant he wasn't done. Not until she understood. "It's like his legs sort of forgot how to walk. So he uses the walker until he remembers."

"So he'll remember?"

"Hopefully his body will remember everything it forgot."

When her father was finally settled, Kate glanced around the makeshift bedroom and her breath caught. Trisha had been right behind her and so had Max. Now they were nowhere in sight. She raced to the kitchen, thinking maybe they were just lagging behind, but the room was empty.

Her heart spun out of control.

Oh, God! Max was a taker. A fun-loving, let-me-show-you-a-good-time guy who believed it was easier to apologize than ask permission. He could have taken Trisha to the yard to play or he could have taken her to his house. He had a pool, and it was hot—

He'd taken her!

She rushed to the living room to tell her parents she was leaving for a minute, not sure how she'd tell them Max had apparently taken Trisha somewhere, when she thought of the family room. Trisha's tea set. Max's desire to get to know their daughter.

Her pounding heart slowed, but her thoughts rolled on. She'd jumped to a bad conclusion because she didn't trust him. This—jumping to conclusions, fearing the worst—was a painful reminder of what life with Max was like. And he was in their life again.

She walked up to the family-room door, saw them sitting at the small plastic table and stopped suddenly as she heard Trisha say, "Mom said Grandpa would be sick for a while." She peeked up at Max, her little face scrunched in a combination of fear and sadness. "I don't want him to be sick."

Looking like a giant, Max shifted on the tiny chair. "He's not really sick anymore. More like recovering."

Trisha's face brightened. "Not sick?"

He winced and took the empty teacup she handed him. He pretended to sip then set the cup down again and said, "He was sick. Very sick. And because he was very sick, certain parts of him don't work as well as they used to."

Trisha's eyes widened in horror. Kate just barely stifled a gasp.

She started to run in and save her child, but Max said, "It's like his legs sort of forgot how to walk. So he uses the walker until he remembers."

"So he'll remember?"

Max's face softened. "Hopefully his body will remember everything it forgot."

When Trisha nodded her understanding, Kate's formerly frantic heart expanded with gratitude. It was so easy to scare a child, easier still to confuse them. Yet Max handled Trisha's fears perfectly. He kept the language on a level a seven-year-old could understand. Drew images she could relate to. And he sat with her, entertaining her, while he spoke. She couldn't have done better herself. Yet she'd doubted him, jumped to a bad conclusion, thought the worst.

Maybe because she was looking for a way to stop her own guilt over the news she had to deliver as soon as she and Max were alone?

There was no sense putting off the inevitable. She stepped into the family room. "Hey, I see you got a new doll."

Max glanced up sharply. "I hope you don't mind."

She ambled over. "We don't mind at all. A present every now and again is a good thing for a little girl. But—" She gave Max a pointed look. "Remember her birthday isn't too far away, so we don't want to go overboard now."

He inclined his head in acceptance. "Makes perfect sense to me."

She eased herself onto one of the chairs and tapped Trisha's soft little hand to get her attention. "Grandma is going to be busy with Grandpa for a while, so I thought it would be a good idea for us to make lunch."

Trisha brightened. "Can I make soup?"

"You can go in the kitchen and get out a can of the kind of soup you want to eat, but I cook."

Trisha growled an "Ah, Mom."

But Kate held her ground and Trisha scampered away.

She faced Max. "I'm sorry about this."

He caught her gaze. "About what?"

Remembering how easy it was to get lost in his perfect blue eyes, she glanced down and toyed with one of the plastic cups. "My dad coming home. I must have been only half paying attention when my mom told me last night there was a possibility he'd come home today." She shrugged. "He's doing so well that he can actually be driven to physical therapy."

"That's great."

"He has very little residual effects from his stroke."

"He was lucky."

"Yes. He was."

And now came the hard part. She swallowed and fortified herself to meet his gaze again. "That means my mom's not going to need us as much as I'd thought."

His eyebrows rose. "Oh?"

She sucked in a breath. "I know I told you that I'd planned to stay three months, which would have given you lots of time to get to know Trisha, but now we'll be going home."

His eyes flickered. But he didn't yell. He barely reacted. He simply said, "Where's home?"

Since she knew he could probably find her with a good investigator, she didn't hesitate. "Tennessee."

"Oh."

His "Oh," was soft, filled with questions and misery, but no anger.

The temptation was strong to put her hand over his, to comfort him, but she kept her hands on her lap. "I'm so sorry."

He shifted on the chair again. "Why do you have to leave? I mean, it sounds like you've already made arrangements to stay three months. Why go back home?"

She shrugged. "Because some of us have to work."

He caught her gaze. "As my child's mother you would never have to work another day in your life. You know that."

Her caution morphed into hope and happiness, confusing her. He was being easy to deal with right now, accommodating, but she knew the other side of this guy. She rose and walked far enough away from him to give herself some distance.

"I happen to like my job."

He eased back on the little chair. "When we were dating you always said you wanted to be a stay-at-home mom."

"I did. But when circumstances shifted and I had to go to work, I discovered I like working."

"So do I."

"Really?" For all the years she'd known him, he'd absolutely hated working, being saddled with an empire, answering to an overbearing, unethical father.

"As I grew more competent, my dad eased off a bit." He shrugged, picked up the Rachel doll and slid it into the packaging again. "I was virtually running the company when he died. I hired really good people as vice presidents and department heads." He grinned at her. "Mostly I only do the jobs I want to do."

She laughed. Then caught herself. This was charming Max. The Max who wanted something. She knew this drill too.

She cleared her throat. "I'm sorry about your dad. I heard when he died. I just never—" Never sent an acknowledgment or sympathy card because she didn't want to be found. She didn't need to say that.

"He was a bully. We all knew it. But my mother loved him and I grieved for what could have been." He shrugged. "But that was two years ago. We've both moved on." He rose from the table. "I can see you and your mom have more going on here than you'd expected. Trisha and I had another nice visit and she's really growing comfortable with me. I don't want to spoil that or interrupt your lunch." He smiled. "So I'll go."

Not wanting to be rude since she'd promised him an afternoon, she said, "You could stay for lunch."

"No." He caught her gaze. "Thanks, though. I'll see you tomorrow." He started for the door, but stopped. "Actually, what I meant to say was can I come by again tomorrow?"

His thoughtfulness surprised her, but the fact that he recognized that he'd sort of bulldozed his way into another visit the next day out-and-out shocked her.

She stuttered a bit when she said, "Sure. One o'clock again." She cautiously took a step toward him. "This time we really will be home."

He laughed and headed for the door. "See you tomorrow."

Rooted to her spot, she watched him go. "See you tomorrow."

She stood there until she heard the front door close, followed by the sound of the electric can opener in the kitchen. Thinking Trisha had gotten bored waiting for her, she dashed into the kitchen to find her mom and Trisha pouring the contents of a soup can into a pot.

Her breath whooshed out. "Wow. I thought Trisha was in here making soup alone."

"Nope." Her mother smiled. "I'm here. We're fine."

"Shouldn't you be with Dad?"

Bev rolled her eyes. "No, he wants to watch Price for a Day. I'm letting him."

Kate laughed, then faced Trisha. She needed some time alone with her mom. "Go put your new Rachel doll away before we eat."

With a happy nod, Trisha darted off.

Bev didn't waste a second. "So, how's Max doing with Trisha?"

Kate reached for the bread to make sandwiches. "Fine." She shook her head. "Actually, he's doing really well. I walked in on him explaining Dad's illness to Trisha. It was adorable."

Her mom stopped midway to the stove. "Oh, no, Katie! I hope you're not going to get sucked into this again."

Kate's skin prickled defensively. Did her mother think she was stupid? "I'm not."

"I mean, when he's sober even I like the guy. And I think he has a right to see Trisha. But he's bad news as a husband."

Kate walked to the toaster. "My memory's not that short, Mom."

And it wasn't. Because the one thing she hadn't seen the day before when she'd visited him in her beautiful former house was the crystal vase her parents had scrimped and saved to buy as a wedding gift for her and Max. She didn't see it because Max had broken it the night she left. He'd been too drunk to remember that it wasn't a gift from his parents, but from hers. To this day he probably didn't even know he'd thrown it against the fireplace and shattered it into a million pieces, along with her heart—and their marriage.

Had he not broken that vase that night, she might have told him she was pregnant. Instead, she'd packed her bags.

Yeah. She remembered exactly how bad a husband Max was.

CHAPTER FIVE

SUNDAY AFTERNOON, when Kate opened the door to Max, she quietly said, "Come in."

Dressed in shorts and a T-shirt with flip-flops, he stepped over the threshold. Then she saw the bag in his hands. Her eyebrows rose. "More gifts?"

"Just another couple of outfits that Annette said no self-respecting Rachel could be without."

Kate laughed. She wasn't going to be charmed, but she couldn't be a bitter ex-wife either. These visits were about Trisha, not her, not even about their bad marriage. Their child. Her mom might be worried, but she had a very good memory. She would be smart this time around.

"Just don't forget we're coming up on her birthday."

She turned to call up the stairs for Trisha but he caught her arm. "So you'll be here for her birthday?"

His hesitant words surprised her. Actually, they sort of hit her in the heart. He might have been a crappy husband, and she might worry about leaving him alone with their daughter, but she intended to play fair. She wouldn't withhold information or permissions, unless warranted. And he should know that.

"Yes. I'm sorry. I should have made myself clear yesterday. We're not staying the entire three months. But we will be staying a few more weeks to help my mom with Dad as he goes through therapy."

He breathed a sigh of relief and Kate turned to the stairway. Expecting him to catch her arm again, so he could get in a couple of arguments about why she should stay more than a few weeks, she paused before she called Trisha. But he didn't say anything else. Didn't even comment on her plans.

She faced him again. "Not going to try to convince me to stay longer?"

"I asked once yesterday. You weren't really open to it. So I'm not going to push. I have enough money and enough private planes that I could visit every weekend if I wanted." He laughed lightly. "I could move beside you if I wanted. So I'll let you make your decisions and I'll make mine."

Confusion rattled through her. She was so accustomed to his persuasions, his sweet-talk, that always ended up with her agreeing to something she didn't want, that she wasn't sure how to react to that. She turned to the stairs. "Trisha!"

"Coming!"

As Trisha clattered down the stairway, Kate's mom walked by with the Scrabble game. "Hey, Max."

"Hey, Bev."

She rattled the box. "Care to join us?"

"Actually, I was hoping Kate, Trisha and I could go to my house to swim this afternoon."

At the foot of the stairs now, Trisha's eyes rounded. "Swim! I love to swim!"

Kate slipped into mother mode. "Trisha, this is one of those things moms like to plan for. We need towels and sunblock."

"I have those in abundance."

"Plus, we'd have to dig out your bathing suit."

Trisha headed up the stairs. "I'll find it."

"But—"

From the living room Kate's dad growled, "Ah, go! It's a

damn hot day and a little girl needs some fun in her life. Not to sit around and watch her grandpa watch TV."

Embarrassed by her dad's outburst, Kate faced Max. "Sorry."

Max chuckled and shook his head. "I think he's funny."

She glanced into the living room, then at Max again. "Yeah, well, I'd like my even-tempered dad back."

"What do the doctors say? Will he ever be his old self again?"

"I'm right here! I can hear you whispering about me."

Kate sighed, leaned in and lowered her voice even more. "Yes, as he regains the strength in his legs and can do all the things he used to do, he'll slip back to normal."

Max whispered, "That's good," and though Kate told herself to pull back, away from him, she didn't. She couldn't. The scent of him drew her closer. She inhaled as inconspicuously as possible and took in the spicy, male, sexy smell that was uniquely Max. She knew that was pathetic, maybe even dangerous. She didn't have enough fingers to count the ways being attracted to him was wrong. But she wasn't really attracted to him. She remembered all the bad things about being Mrs. Maxwell Montgomery. She just loved the way he looked, the way he smelled, the physical way he made her feel.

Emotionally, though, he was public enemy number one. She knew that. She wouldn't let something physical turn into something emotional again. But she just couldn't stop the urge for that scent.

Max put his hand on her shoulder and casually directed her up the stairs. "Go. Grab your swimsuit and your sunblock. I'll entertain your dad for a few minutes."

The touch of his hand on her shoulder all but melted her bones. She'd been on a few dates the past couple of years, but she'd never had another lover. Now she knew why. No man could ever really take Max's place.

She raced up the stairs, heart in her throat. She'd told herself not to sniff him but she had, and then he'd touched her and she'd gotten all melty. And a new lesson had been learned. It wasn't safe to get too close. Not even when she thought she was strong. There was something about him that called to her. It was basic, elemental. Purely animal instinct. Not something she could explain or control. But for that very reason she couldn't toy with it.

At the top of the stairs, she heard Max's muffled voice followed quickly by her dad's gruff guffaw of laughter. Since his stroke, her dad had smiled. He'd put on a brave face. But he hadn't laughed. Max, the guy her dad had absolutely, positively hated since year two of their marriage when he'd started drinking heavily, had made him laugh.

She turned and glanced downstairs just in time to see her mom coming out of the living room, tray in hand.

"What's up?"

Her mom quickly glanced up. "Nothing."

"Daddy laughed."

"Oh, that ridiculous Max told him a dirty joke."

She smiled. "Really?"

"A silly one at that."

"Okay, I'll gather our stuff quickly so we can get out of your hair."

Her mom waved a hand. "Don't hurry. Let's give your dad a few minutes of guy time for a change. He is surrounded by women, you know."

With only Kate and her mom in her dad's life, he had always been a little desperate for male companionship. Even his only grandchild was a girl. "Yeah. He is."

"So as long as Max is up for entertaining, let's let him."

Kate walked back down the hall to the room she and Trisha were sharing and found her daughter already dressed in her swimming suit. "You could have just packed your backpack. Your dad has a pool house."

Her eyes grew large with excitement. "Really?"

"Yeah." And it suddenly dawned on Kate that "Charming Max" might be back again. Only stealthier than he had been a few years ago. He'd show Trisha his gorgeous house, his beautiful pool, all the electronic games he had—not to mention the pool table and foosball table—and Trisha wouldn't ever want to go home.

Maybe they shouldn't go swimming?

And have him stay here and charm her dad some more? Her dad might hate Max but he was vulnerable. Given enough time could Max charm him onto his side? Maybe persuade him into talking Kate into moving home from Tennessee?

Max could charm anyone into anything.

She glanced uneasily at the drawer containing her bathing suit. She was sort of damned if she did and damned if she didn't. Still, Trisha was already in her suit. Plus, she was different now. Her dad might be vulnerable to Max's charisma, but she wasn't the starry-eyed co-ed Max had wooed.

She faced Trisha with a smile. "Let me rub on some sunblock before we go."

Nodding happily, Trisha skipped over. A few minutes later, slathered with the sunblock Kate found in the medicine cabinet, Trisha left the room. Kate packed her suit in a little beach bag, along with the sunblock, and made her way down the stairs, determined to handle Max.

When she reached the bottom of the steps, she peeked into the living room and saw that Max was holding Trisha, who had her arm around his neck. Yeah, he was definitely winning points with his daughter. But she was the adult. In control. They would be fine.

In the driveway, he motioned for everybody to get into his Range Rover but she declined.

"I'll drive us. Trisha still uses a car seat. Plus, if I drive us you won't have to come back with us when we're done swimming."

He set Trisha down in front of her car. "Okay." Then he walked back to his Range Rover, climbed in and drove off.

Her eyes narrowed. That was at least the second time he should have argued or cajoled, but hadn't. But this time she realized that might be part of his plan. Be so nice and accommodating that she'd let her guard down. She snorted a laugh. He was going to be one disappointed guy. She couldn't even smell him without getting weak-kneed. She most certainly could not let her guard down.

She hustled Trisha and her backpack into the back seat and buckled her in. Then she tossed her own beach bag into the passenger seat and they shoved off.

When they reached his house, Max was already by the pool, wearing blue trunks that somehow made his blue eyes appear bluer. Dark hair unapologetically covered his muscled chest. His abs were tight, the muscles defined. His arms, too, were bigger, muscled, as if he now regularly went to the gym. He wasn't the lean boy he'd been while they were married. He was buff. Add that to his good looks, and her mouth watered.

Oh, man. This was so not a good idea.

When Trisha approached, he scooped her off her feet and hugged her, as naturally as any father would. All thoughts of his good looks were forgotten as her heart swelled. Trisha had never missed having a dad, but she was at the stage where having a dad would be important. Plus, she needed a male role model and her granddad lived so far from Tennessee that he wasn't an influence. If Max really would visit, Trisha would benefit so much from having him in her life.

As long as he didn't start drinking again.

That was the kicker.

That was the thing that mitigated his good looks. She

couldn't be drooling over the guy when she had to be alert, watching for signs that Max was in trouble, protecting her daughter.

She ambled over to them. "Hey."

"Hey." He glanced at her shorts and T-shirt. "You're not ready."

"I can be ready in two minutes."

"Ah, Mom! We have to wait?"

She almost said, "You can wait two minutes," because she was so accustomed to parenting alone. But Max was Trisha's other parent. He would be in her life. Kate needed to let that begin happening.

"No. You and your dad can go in." She pointed toward the pool house. "I'll just go change and be out in a minute."

Max turned Trisha in his arms so she faced him. "Can you swim?"

She nodded, but Kate proudly said, "She's on the junior swim team at her school."

Max grinned. "Really?"

Trisha nodded eagerly.

And Max tossed her into the pool. Kate's heart all but exploded from shock. But Trisha sputtered to the surface like a pro, as Max jumped in beside her.

Her heart spun to life again, and she headed toward the pool house, but Max's laughter stopped her. They'd had this pool when they'd lived here and the only time he'd ever gone anywhere near it was when they hosted a pool party. Today he was splashing around with their daughter, enjoying himself. His wet black hair glistened in the sunlight. His blue eyes glittered with happiness. And there wasn't a bottle of vodka around. No one to impress. Hell, he wasn't even trying to impress her.

Truth be told, he sort of ignored her.

Telling herself that was for the best, she ducked into the

pool house, changed into her old red one-piece suit and made her way to the pool. At the stairs, she dipped a toe into the water.

"Ah, come on. That's no way to get into a pool."

She glanced up and saw Max watching her. His gaze took a quick stroll down her body and back up again, but that was enough to kick-start her hormones. Heat pooled low in her belly. Her chest tingled. Pride almost made her smile, as one thought rolled through her brain. He wasn't as indifferent to her as she'd thought.

But that wasn't good. She didn't want to be attracted to him and she didn't want him attracted to her.

So why was her heart tripping over itself in her chest?

Chemistry.

She reminded herself that their attraction was purely biological and remembered enough of their past to snuff it out.

Then he stood. Water cascaded down his chest, making rivulets in the thick forest of black hair, tumbling to swimming trunks that clung to his lean hips.

This time her mouth went dry.

Oh, yeah, they definitely had chemistry and that definitely clouded her judgment. But she could handle this. She had to handle this.

"Yeah, Mummy, dive!"

"It's not deep enough to dive."

Trisha pointed to the diving board. "On this end it is."

Kate sighed. "Trisha, there's a reason I got you swimming lessons as a baby. Your mom isn't much of a swimmer."

Max glanced over. "As I recall you were perfectly fine as a swimmer."

She had been. Living here those five years, spending long afternoons in this same pool, she'd gotten very good. Not good enough or brave enough to dive, but good enough that she wouldn't drown.

"Bet if I threw you in, it would all come back to you."

She took a step back. "Don't even think about it."

Max began walking to her side of the pool. "You have until the count of ten. Then I pick you up and toss you in like I did Trisha." He took a step. "One." Another step. "Two." A third step. "Three."

Her heart began to thud. Not because of her fear of being tossed into the water. Visions of him sliding his arm beneath her knees, holding her against his furry chest flooded her. That was no way for them to avoid their chemistry.

"All right!"

She scurried down the ladder. Not giving him the chance to touch her, she slid into the water. Using her elementary, I-taught-myself-how-to-swim stroke, she glided over to Trisha.

"Happy now?"

Trisha threw her arms around her neck and kissed her cheek with a loud smack. Kate laughed.

Swimming away, Trisha said, "Let's play catch."

Max grabbed a beach ball and tossed it at her. She caught it and tossed it to her mom. Instead of catching it, though, Kate swatted it to him. He missed it.

Realizing she was changing games from catch to volley-ball, he said, "I wasn't ready."

"Well, it's not like you go to jail or anything," Kate said, laughing, shielding her eyes from the sun with her hand. "You just have to get the ball."

He did. Not only was he the one who'd missed it, but also his heart had slammed into his ribs when she'd laughed and he needed a minute. He'd done a reasonably credible job of holding back his attraction to her, but seeing her in the old red swimsuit had brought back an avalanche of memories. Not all of them were good. But those that were took his mind and some of his other body parts to happier times.

She'd been a wonderful wife, an eager partner in bed.

And even though he kept reminding himself that he'd blown that, her sweet personality called to him. If there was ever a woman who'd give somebody a second chance, it was Kate.

But if there was ever a person who didn't deserve a second chance, it was him.

It would be wrong to take advantage of her sweetness. Especially since she clearly didn't feel anything for him. Except maybe suspicion.

Which he deserved.

He hoisted himself out of the pool, scooped up the beach ball and threw it at Trisha. Obviously knowing the game, she tossed it in the air and swatted it to her mom. Kate swiveled and batted it in his direction. He stretched to meet it and hit it to Trisha.

The game went on with only a few misses. The person who'd failed to hit the ball had to get out of the pool to retrieve it. But after ten minutes, Trisha got bored. Without a word of explanation, she ducked under the water and swam away.

Max stood staring at the spot where she had been. Kate waded over. "She's about to turn seven. Her attention span leaves a lot to be desired."

"So I see."

They stood in the four-foot water, watching as she climbed the ladder and then scooted to the diving board.

"Look at me!"

As she scrambled along the board, Kate said, "Get used to those words. They are her favorites."

He faced her. "Look at me?"

"Yes." Her eyes on Trisha, Kate's face glowed with love. Her eyes shone like two emeralds. Her full lips bowed upward. "She's definitely the star of her own life. Sort of a real-life reality show."

Max's heart slowed to a crawl. The world around him seemed to move to slow motion. This was a moment a man never forgot. Seeing the look of love on the face of the mother of his child. He'd missed Trisha's birth. He'd missed that first look that passed between mother and daughter. But he saw that love now. And it humbled him.

He'd forced her to parent alone. He'd forced her to go through a pregnancy alone. He'd forced her out of his life.

The words "I'm sorry" caught in his throat. He'd already told her he was sorry. Saying it again might cheapen it. But in that second he was sorrier than even he knew he could feel, if only because being with Trisha and Kate was making him finally begin to see the scope of what he'd lost.

Suddenly the water around him exploded as Trisha landed from her dive. She sputtered up beside him. "You didn't watch!"

Embarrassment stole through him. Kate might not have seen him staring at her, but Trisha had. "Sorry."

Kate waved her hand, motioning Trisha back to the board. "Go again. This time Daddy will watch."

Daddy.

The word tightened his chest, filled his heart with something unbearably brilliant. He was in his pool with the woman he'd always adored and his daughter. His daughter.

He didn't deserve this.

Kate nudged his arm. "Watch this time," she said with a laugh. "Or we'll be here all day."

"I could stay here all day." He swallowed the lump in his throat. "My God, I'm sorry. I'm sorry I missed her birth. I'm sorry I didn't help you through the pregnancy. I'm so sorry."

She licked her lips and turned away. "You'll be even sorrier if you miss her second dive."

Her voice was sort of light, as if she'd tried to make the moment funny and failed. Pain twisted through him. She didn't want any more apologies. He didn't blame her. But even knowing he deserved her indifference didn't stop it from hurting.

The water around him splashed again and he squeezed his eyes shut. He'd missed Trisha's dive again.

She surged out of the water. "Did you see?"

He winced. It would have been so easy to lie, but that was a slippery slope, a slope he vowed he'd never go down again. "I saw you land."

"Dad!"

Once again, Kate motioned her out of the water. "You love to dive. It's not as if it's a hardship for you to go one more time."

Trisha giggled, swam to the edge of the pool and climbed onto the board. "Stop looking at Mom and watch this time."

Like a kid caught with his hand in a cookie jar, he actually felt his face redden. "I'm watching! Don't lollygag on the board this time."

She laughed, ran down the board and flew into the air, landing a few feet in front of him.

As she paddled to the surface, Kate leaned toward him. "Applause is always welcome."

He burst out laughing. As Trisha pushed out of the water, he clapped. So did Kate.

"You saw!"

"It was great!" It was great. Perfect.

"I'll go again."

As she swam to the edge, Kate quickly faced him. "It was you who told me not to think of the past. So I'm going to remind you of what you said. Don't think of the past. Not when she's with you. She's too young to know about our troubles. When she gets older we'll tell her I left because we couldn't get along, because that's true. We couldn't get along. And maybe someday when she's old enough to really understand you can tell her the rest. But for right now, this is her time to have a daddy. Don't spoil it."

He licked his suddenly dry lips. "Okay." He sucked in a breath. "I get it. I also realize you're giving me a great gift. A gift I don't deserve. And I'm trying to accept it. But something inside me feels like we're missing something." He rubbed his hand along the back of his neck. "Or maybe doing something wrong."

"It's not wrong to keep that secret from Trisha. And I'm not suggesting we keep it forever. Just until she's old enough to understand."

That wasn't what Max had been referring to. In a back-handed way, he was trying to talk about her indifference to him, hoping, for what he wasn't sure. But it didn't matter. Kate turned and swam away, ending the conversation. She hoisted herself up the ladder and walked over to the chaise where she'd draped her towel.

"I think I'll just sit here and watch for a few minutes."

Trisha raced across the diving board and tossed herself into the water, which splashed Max.

He was gaining a daughter, a beautiful gift. So why did he suddenly feel compelled to force Kate to talk about them?

Because being around Kate brought the reality of losing her to startling life.

All these years he must have believed that if she ever came back into his life, he'd get a second chance, because in the nearly eight years she was gone he'd never had another serious relationship. But after her reaction, he now knew with absolute certainty that there would be no second chance for him.

CHAPTER SIX

TRISHA WAS PLAYING in the front yard when Max arrived the next day. He stepped out of his Mercedes, ambled over.

She sat on a rich patch of grass beside an oak tree, combing the hair of her new Rachel doll. Sunlight streamed through the leafy branches above her. Birds chirped, but otherwise the street was silent. Various-sized dolls sat in a circle around her, as if they were having a coffee klatch.

"What are you doing?"

She looked up. "Hey, Dad."

His heart only stuttered a bit this time. He was growing accustomed to hearing her sweet voice call him Dad. In a way it saddened him. He didn't want anything about being a parent to be common, ordinary. But it also pleased him. She was so comfortable with him, so accepting, that it made his acceptance of the loss of Kate's love just a little easier to bear.

"Where's your mom?"

"Inside with Gram and Grandpa."

He stooped down beside her. "Is everything okay?"

She shrugged. "I don't think Grandpa likes oatmeal."

He laughed. "Most men don't."

She said nothing.

"Are you okay?"

She shrugged again. "I don't like sad Grandpa."

"Why don't I go in and check things out?"

She nodded eagerly. So eagerly, he assumed it was the right thing to do. But when he got to the door, he hesitated. What did he think he was? Their savior? He snorted a laugh. He wasn't anybody's savior. But he was a man, and he had made Dennis laugh the day before. Maybe Dennis could relate to him?

With that thought, he took a long breath and opened the front door. "Anybody home?"

Bev said, "We're in here, Max."

His gaze automatically swung to Kate.

Placing a pillow behind her dad's head, she smiled mechanically at him. "Hello, Max."

He fought the disappointment that swelled at her lackluster greeting. "Hey."

"Trisha's outside. Why don't you go join her?"

Awkward, he rubbed his hand along the back of his neck. "Actually, I was just with her." He winced. "She sort of…" Deciding just to bite the bullet and do as he'd promised his daughter, he glanced at Dennis. "Well, she's worried about you."

"There's not a damned thing to be worried about except two fussing women." He shifted on the bed. "I should be in a chair. My therapist wants me in a chair. She wants me to practice walking with the walker. Which means I could be going to the kitchen for my own glass of water now and again." He glared at his wife. "But she won't let me."

Kate's eyebrows rose in surprise. "Is that true, Mom?"

"Yes. But Melanie must be wrong." Bev fussed with Dennis's pillows again. "The man had a stroke ten days ago for God's sake. He should be in bed."

"Not necessarily," Max said, and from the glare that came to him from Bev, he wished he hadn't. Still, he was in now. "Things have changed in medicine in the past few years."

The room became deathly silent.

Finally, Kate glanced at him. Apparently seeing his misery, she faced her mom. "He's right, Mom." She ran her fingers along the edge of the comforter covering her dad. "It's summer and we have him wrapped in blankets. The therapist wants him in a chair and we've got him in bed." She sucked in a breath. "I know what we're doing. We're being overprotective because we're scared. But if the therapist really said he could be in a chair and practicing walking—"

"She said I needed to practice walking," her dad growled.

"Then he should be doing as she says."

Her mom deflated. "It doesn't seem right."

"But it is right," Dennis said, his voice softening as he grabbed Bev's hand. "I'm sorry I scared you, but I'm going to be fine."

Uncomfortable hanging around for their private moment, Max motioned toward the door. "I'll just go back outside with Trisha."

Kate slid away from her dad's bed. "I'll go too."

Max waited for her at the front door, which he opened for her. The second they were on the porch, he said, "I'm sorry."

She blew her breath out gustily. "If you keep apologizing for every little thing that goes wrong, you're going to drive us both nuts. You've gotta stop saying you're sorry."

"Actually, what I have to stop doing is interfering."

She peeked over, sent him a confused look, then quickly glanced away. "Give yourself some credit. You made him laugh yesterday. Today you gave him the opening to help me see that my mom and I were overfussing. Your interfering was good."

He scratched his chin. "I hope so because I backhandedly promised our daughter I'd try to bring back her not-sad grandpa."

"So that's why you came in."

"And why I butted in."

"Understandable." She started down the stairs and called to Trisha. "So, how's Rachel's hair?"

"It's still too much."

As they walked toward Trisha, she leaned into Max and whispered. "She means too thick. I think she's going to give poor Rachel a crew cut."

He laughed to cover the way his breath stuttered when the scent of her hair drifted to him.

"Don't laugh. She'll be sorry when she has a hairless doll and all her friends' dolls are still gorgeous."

"We'll just get her another one."

She gasped and caught his forearm, stopping him. Tingles skittered up his arm. Not because she'd touched him but because she'd done it so naturally, so easily, just as she had when they were married.

"No. No. No. We do not buy her everything she wants. We especially don't replace things she ruins. She has to learn lessons from these things."

She stepped closer, squeezed his arm. Arousal roared through him, tightening his chest, heating his blood to scalding, sending a river of molten need through him. His gaze shot to her pretty green eyes. They were neutral. Not happy. Not sad. Neutral. She hadn't touched him because she wanted contact. The fingers on his forearm were a reflex leftover from an unhappy time.

An unhappy time. A time he didn't want her to remember.

He shifted away. "Right. Got it."

His movement left her hand suspended. A few seconds passed in silence as she glanced down at it, then up at him, then she pivoted away and all but ran over to Trisha.

"I wanna go inside."

Kate bent and picked up a doll. "Okay. We can take the troop into the family room."

"Is Grandpa happy?"

"He's better."

Trish's mouth bowed down into an upside down U. "I don't think he likes me."

"He loves you!" Kate assured her, stooping down to run her hand down Trisha's soft brown hair.

"How could he not love you?" Max asked. "You're adorable."

But as he crouched down beside Kate and Trisha, Kate hastily rose. "We'll go in the back door. We can slide into the family room without Grandma and Grandpa even noticing we're coming inside."

With that she bent down and swiped up another doll. Trish caught three in her little arms and Max gathered the remaining three. Kate headed for the back porch with Trisha on her heels and he followed them.

But the afternoon didn't go well. Dennis and Bev hadn't really come to a truce about his health because she went back to fussing over him. So Dennis closed the pocket doors in the living room and wouldn't let anyone in. With the tension in the house, Trisha couldn't seem to settle. One minute she wanted to play tea party, the next she wanted to watch TV. But one thing was clear to Max. She didn't want him around. After an hour of her ignoring him, even relegating him to the sofa so she could have a private tea party with the queen, Max rose.

"I think I'll go."

Kate followed him into the hall. When they were out of earshot of the family room, she said, "Don't take it personally. She's just restless. We're in a strange town. Her grandpa is sick and she spent the first week of our visit in a hospital room."

"And she met me."

Kate stepped closer and once again put her hand on his forearm. Clearly, her upset over her dad had caused her to forget their prior encounter like this one. Preoccupied, she reverted to natural, spontaneous behavior. "And she's spent every afternoon with you because she likes you. I think she just needs a break."

He swallowed, wishing that instead of focusing on his anger with his dad and his half brother when he'd stopped drinking, he'd also dealt with his feelings about Kate leaving. Because now, when she touched him, he still reacted. In his head, he knew she wanted nothing to do with him and he should want nothing to do with her—if only out of respect for her decision. But his heart and his hormones simply weren't on board. They were eight years in the past, remembering how things could have been, and yearning like hungry pups. Even though he knew she was only standing close and touching him because she was a nice person who liked physical contact, who was too preoccupied with her dad to remember she shouldn't be touching him.

He stepped away. "Should I not come over tomorrow?"

She caught his gaze. "This time tomorrow she'll probably be perfectly fine."

He sighed. "Okay."

She once again breached the distance between them, and once again consolingly laid her hand on his forearm. "I swear. She's just having a bad day."

Unwanted needs sprang to vivid life. The urge to run his fingers through her hair, or along her chin, to feel her skin, to appreciate her softness, to have the privileges he'd had eight years ago, nudged him on. He stepped closer, willing her to look at him.

It was then that she must have realized she was touching him again because she pulled her hand back as if it had been burned.

Their gazes caught and clung. Since she'd been home, he'd believed she was angry or indifferent; he'd never once considered that even an ounce of their chemistry had survived for her. But staring into her crystal-green eyes, he saw a spark flicker to life.

She took another pace back and he stood befuddled. Hope and curiosity battled common sense. Common sense won. Even if she was attracted to him, she didn't want to be. She'd just about come right out and said that the day before.

She smiled weakly. "I'll see you tomorrow."

He released the breath he didn't even realize he'd been holding. "Okay."

Three steps took him to the door. He opened it. Walked outside. And stood on her porch.

He couldn't stop thinking about the spark in her eyes. Surely he'd imagined it. It was, after all, only a spark.

But what if it was more?

Kate stood on the other side of the door, sucking in much-needed oxygen. She'd touched him. Several times. And he'd noticed, but he'd had the good grace not to say anything to her.

She combed her fingers through her hair and headed for the kitchen, telling herself that she hadn't felt anything when her fingers very casually slid to his arm, so it was nothing. She was just a touchy person. She even backed that up at dinner by noticing how many times she touched her mom to get her attention, the way she touched Trisha, the times she touched her dad.

Of course, they were all people she loved.

No. No. She would not let herself think that way. She had not touched Max out of affection. She'd caught his arm once to stop him. Twice to get his attention. That was all.

The next day Max called, surprising her, and her damned heart leapt to her throat, the way it had when he'd called when they were dating.

"How about if we swim again this afternoon?"

"I don't know—" She took a breath. Why was she suddenly going all crazy around him?

"Let's do this for Trisha. And your parents. Give Trisha a bit of a break from them and them a break from her."

There wasn't one hint of anything in his voice except for concern for his daughter. They'd had a terrible day the day before and he was only trying to make sure this visit was a good one. If she made a big deal out of spending time alone with him at his house, then he'd know their chemistry was starting to rear up for her. And that's when he'd take advantage. After touching him the day before—and him noticing—she had to show him she was indifferent to him. Even if she was starting to worry that she wasn't. "Actually, that might not be a bad idea."

"Great. Just bring her to the house around two. We'll have a nice afternoon."

At five minutes till two, she had herself fortified for an afternoon of rebuffing him. Or at the very least demonstrating that she was not having trouble with their chemistry. Because she wasn't. She stood by her conclusion that those touches the day before were reflex. And even if she found him attractive, that was normal. He was attractive. She'd be blind not to notice. So she was not nuts. Not giving in to their chemistry. She was normal.

They arrived at his house to find Max dragging the net through the pool water to clean it. He wore red trunks, exposing his gorgeous chest and tight abs and everything inside her softened. Which she'd already decided was fine. He was a gorgeous man. She was a normal woman. She could find him attractive. As long as she didn't act on it.

Walking over to the pool, her hand on Trisha's shoulder, she called, "Hi! We're here."

He turned, set down the net and strode over to meet them halfway. "Hi."

Proper and polite, she said, "Thanks for inviting us." Then their gazes caught and her tummy plummeted. It was one thing to be attracted to him physically, but those eyes of his. They seemed to go the whole way to his soul, to make her feel that she was the only woman in the universe—

She stepped back. That was not the way to show him their chemistry didn't matter.

Trisha raised her hands in the air for him to pick her up. "Throw me in."

He happily obliged, reaching down to grab her by the waist and toss her into the water. Laughing, she sputtered up and all thoughts of Max and his good looks were forgotten. After the morning they'd had with her dad, her mom and the therapist, hearing Trisha laugh was like a soothing balm.

"Maybe this was a good idea."

"Of course it was."

His smooth voice flowed over her, setting off fireworks inside her, frustrating her. She had to be with Max and Trisha for these visits. She refused to leave her alcoholic ex-husband alone with their daughter until he proved himself. They'd also needed to get out of the house and away from her nervous mother and grouchy dad. But suddenly, being with him wasn't simple anymore. Every time she looked at him, something happened in her belly. When their gazes caught, she wanted to swoon. Now his voice was scrambling her pulse.

With a quick turn, he propelled himself into the pool. Trisha laughed when he sent water flying in all directions. He ducked under the surface, caught her around the waist, hoisted her out of the water and sent her flying into the deep end. She squealed with delight, landed with a splash, then popped up again.

Kate kicked off her shoes and slipped off the cover-up. This was the point where she had to make a stand. Or maybe draw a line. They didn't need her to have fun on these visits and she didn't want to get sucked into the vortex of trouble that was an attraction to Max Montgomery. Especially not when there was an easy fix.

"You two are having such a good time that I think I'll just sit here on the chaise for a minute."

Trisha whined, "Ah, Mom!"

Max turned and studied her face. If he was looking for signs of lying, he wouldn't find them. She hadn't lied. She'd never lie. He'd taught her how bad even white lies could be.

As Trisha scrambled out of the water, over to the diving board, he waded to the side of the pool in front of her.

"What's up?"

The genuine concern she heard in his voice sent her pulse scrambling again. Still, there was no reason to be nervous. She might want to be away from him because of an unwanted attraction, but she didn't need to mention that. She had plenty of other reasons to want a few minutes to herself while he entertained Trisha.

"Nothing. I could just use a break. We had a busy morning with the therapist. And Mom's still not handling things well. Which upsets Trisha."

He nodded to their daughter who was scampering across the diving board. "She's over it."

"She's not the one who ran around trying to soothe everybody's hurt feelings."

He studied her for a few seconds, then floated back a bit. "You're right. You probably could use a break. Trisha and I will be fine."

He turned to dive under, and she nearly breathed a sigh of relief, but he pivoted around again. "Would you like a book or something?"

Annoyed by his persistence, particularly when it caused an unwanted tug on her heart, she was a little more forceful this time. "All I want is to close my eyes and not hear anything but the sound of my child's laughter and contentment for a few minutes."

But instead of being forceful, her voice had come out angry and maybe even snide. He took a step back. "Okay. Great. Fine."

As he swam away, she closed her eyes. She might have been snide but he'd gotten the message. She wasn't going to dwell on something that actually got her what she wanted. Away from him.

Max's conversation with Trisha drifted to her. "Wanna have a diving contest?"

"You'll beat me."

"So you're chicken?"

Trisha groaned. "I'm not chicken. You're bigger."

"The diving board doesn't know the difference."

Kate opened one eye and watched as he swam to the far end of the pool and hoisted himself out. Though she'd just barked at him, he acted as if everything was fine. For Trisha. Which was exactly how it was supposed to be.

Trisha quickly followed him and for the next fifteen minutes they executed every kind of dive Max could come up with, including a cannonball. Eventually, they grabbed the beach ball and began to bat it back and forth. Having fun. Not needing her around. Not even wanting her around.

And she'd yelled at him for asking her if she wanted a book.

Feeling foolish, Kate left the chaise and sat on the edge of the pool, dangling her feet in the shallow water. He'd truly wanted a nice afternoon with his daughter and like a shrew, she'd snapped at him. But she was dealing with a lot. Not just Trisha and Max. But her parents. Her dad's recovery. A bossy therapist.

By the time they were done diving, she had waded in.

He swam over. "Feeling better?"

She swished her hand along the surface of the blue water. "Actually, I feel a bit stupid."

"Really?"

"My father's recovering nicely. My mother is simply over-reacting. It will all work out eventually. I should just chill."

"You're missing a few steps in that story. You reconnected with your ex and now he's in your daughter's life. There's a lot of stress in there."

She laughed. "You do realize you're talking about yourself?"

Trisha padded along the side of the pool and stooped down to be at eye level with them. "I'm hungry."

"Trisha!"

"Hey, she's my daughter. She should be able to ask her dad for food." He made his way to the ladder and climbed out. "I have Fudgsicles and ice cream. But that's about it." He reached down and lifted her into his arms. "Men don't usually stock up on junk food. We expect women to supply it. Luckily, I have a maid who shops for me."

Trisha giggled, but as she turned to go into the house, Kate scrambled to the edge of the pool. "Get a towel!" She grabbed the ladder and began climbing out. "Get two towels! Trisha, you know better than to go into the house wet!"

Trisha scooted down, took a towel from the chaise, swiped it over her wet limbs, wrapped it around her waist and headed for the French doors into the family room.

Max called out to her, "The maid's name is Mrs. Gentry. Tell her you want a snack."

Trisha nodded and darted inside.

He reached over to the chaise where he'd laid his big white towel. "I'd forgotten what a stickler you were for the rules."

She gaped at him. "Stickler for rules? Wet people drying off isn't stickling. It's common sense."

She started after Trisha, but he looped his arm around her

shoulders. Telling herself he was only being friendly and she didn't want to inadvertently yell at him again, she stopped herself from stiffening.

"I don't see your towel."

With a gurgle of disgust, she ducked out from under his hold, caught her towel, dried off and wrapped it around her waist as she walked back over to him.

He put his arm across her shoulders again. And again she told herself to stop being persnickety. But this time warmth flooded her, along with a barrage of memories. She longed to close her eyes and steep herself in them. Not just the images of the good times in their marriage, but also the feelings.

"Better. Now we're all in towels."

She laughed, glad he'd brought her back to reality as they walked to the French door, but when he paused in front of it—in that split second when he turned slightly to reach for the doorknob—their gazes collided.

And suddenly it was twelve years ago. When they were young and in love and happy.

She told herself to move out from under his arm. Mentally willed him to step away from her. Instead, they stayed where they were. Quiet. Waiting. Watching each other.

Which was not good.

"So are you going to open the door?"

He tilted his head as he continued to study her. "In a minute."

Fear and unwanted excitement hit her simultaneously. It was so wrong to be this close, and yet it felt so damned good. "And we're waiting for what?"

"I—" His breath heaved out on a heavy sigh. "In the past eight years, I haven't been in love."

That surprised her so much she laughed. "What?"

"I haven't been able to fall in love and I blame you."

"Me?"

"I was so in love with you, Kate, that when I lost you I sobered up. But I also knew you were gone for good, so I had to move on. But as hard as I tried to fall for someone else, I couldn't. To make myself feel better, I told myself that you and I had something legendary. A love beyond what other people feel."

It was the sweetest thing anyone had ever said to her, but it was also dangerous. "Max—"

He put his hands on her shoulders and forced her to look at him. "I need to know there was a reason for the long years I spent alone, yearning for something I wasn't even sure existed."

His hands fell from her shoulders to her wrists, then slid back up again. The feeling was so exquisite, she shuddered and her eyes drifted shut.

"Ah. There it is."

What? Her eyes popped open and she gaped at him. "What are you doing!"

Painfully honest, he said, "I just wanted to see it again."

She jumped away from him. "You wanted a reaction?"

When he didn't answer she pointed her finger at him. "That was stupid. Wrong! Don't ever try anything like that again."

She opened the door and headed inside. But her hands trembled and her legs were rubber, making her angry with herself.

Why couldn't she just not be attracted to this guy?

CHAPTER SEVEN

KATE SPENT EXACTLY fifteen more minutes at Max's house. Just long enough for Trisha to eat a Fudgsicle. Then she wrapped her daughter in a dry towel and raced home.

Her cheeks were flushed. Her body tingled. She would never, ever be alone with him again! The idiot!

In her bathtub that night, she finally calmed down. Odd as her conclusion seemed, she believed she'd figured out what he'd been doing. Testing what she'd known all along. Before he'd started drinking, they'd had something special. She didn't know why he thought he had to test it. She'd always known. But she also knew he'd ruined their marriage, destroyed their relationship, obliterated her feelings. There was no going back. If he tried anything on his next visit with Trisha, she would tell him that. She would not make a big deal out of this. She would be logical. But she would set him straight.

Because if she couldn't get him to behave, there'd be no more visitation. She would not risk him charming her into a relationship again.

But the next two days, Max couldn't clear his schedule to spend afternoons with Trisha. Which negated the possibility that he'd been trying to charm her. If he wanted to charm her, he'd do what he'd done when she was at university. He'd always be around.

Relieved of the burden of that possibility, she felt much better when he came to the door for his next visit.

"Come in, Max."

"Thanks." He glanced around, obviously edgy. When he saw they were alone, he caught her gaze. "Look. I know you said you didn't want any more apologies, but I need to say I'm sorry for what I did the other day…so I'm saying it."

The sincere expression on his handsome face squeezed her heart. Which was fine. Honest emotional response to their situation was not uncontrollable chemistry—

She frowned. When had that switched? A few days ago chemistry was fine, but emotion wasn't. Now, she was allowing herself to feel things?

"Apology accepted, as long as you don't try anything like that again."

"I won't."

She turned away. Needing Trisha to run interference before he said anything else, she called upstairs, "Honey, your dad is here."

Trisha came bouncing down the steps. "Hey, Dad!"

He scooped her up. "Hey, kid. We gonna have a tea party?"

He headed for the family room and Kate followed, but at the juncture that would have taken her to the family room or the kitchen, she hesitated. The purpose of her being around when he visited was to keep Trisha safe. But since they were in her parents' house and he'd been very, very good with their daughter on all his other visits, there was no reason for her to be in the room with them anymore. She still wanted to be in the same house, but there was no reason to be in the same room.

She turned toward the kitchen. "You go ahead and take Trisha into the family room. I'm trying out a new recipe. Something the therapist suggested to help keep Dad's cholesterol down. If you need me, you'll know where to find me."

"You're not coming with us?"

"No." She almost faced him again, but realized she didn't need to give an explanation. Talking too much, getting to know each other again, fed those old feelings. It was time for that to stop.

He said, "Okay," and she walked into the kitchen.

She took her time preparing the casserole. When it was ready, she set it on top of the stove because it was actually too early to put it in the oven. Bored, she drummed her fingers on the kitchen counter. She could go check on them—

Just the thought filled her with trepidation. She knew what it was like to be involved with him, to have more than chemistry, to have real feelings. And she didn't want to go there again. He was perfectly capable with Trisha. She didn't need to watch over him like an overbearing boss—like his dad.

That thought made her even more uncomfortable. Nobody could do overbearing the way Brandon Montgomery could, and she absolutely didn't want to think of herself treating Max that way. She sat at the table again and began going through the recipes the therapist had given her mom. Choosing three that looked practical and promising, she prepared a shopping list. That took twenty minutes.

A happy squeal from Trisha told her that they were still in the family room. There was no reason to worry. And staying away was the right thing to do. He deserved time alone with his daughter. And she didn't want to be confused anymore. Technically, she was setting things right with this situation. Ex-wives and ex-husbands weren't supposed to mix and mingle.

In fact, she could look at the time he spent entertaining Trisha as personal time. Time she could do something she wanted to do. Like read. How long had it been since she'd had even ten minutes to read? Weeks. Since she'd gotten here she hadn't even opened a book.

She shoved off her chair and headed for the foyer stairway. She had two books on her nightstand. Either one of them would do.

But when she passed her father's makeshift bedroom in the living room and saw it was empty, she stopped. That was odd. With her mom still having a bit of a problem with hovering, her parents rarely left the living room.

It piqued her curiosity enough that she checked the front porch to see if they were sitting on the swing. They weren't.

She frowned. Maybe they were on the back porch?

She ambled back to the kitchen and peered out at the lawn furniture on the back porch. No one.

Just then another squeal erupted from the family room. Trisha shouted, "Grandpa, you can't do that!"

Kate spun around. Her parents were in the family room? Maybe Max had gone?

Surprised, she headed out of the kitchen, but stopped dead in the doorway to the family room. There on the little plastic chairs were her parents, Max and Trisha, playing the junior version of Scrabble.

Her dad saw her first, "Hey, Kate."

She took a step inside. "Hey."

"Trisha's whipping the tar out of us."

"I see." She did see. Not only did Max instinctively know to let their daughter win, but also her parents were very comfortable with him. Like family.

She swallowed. She enjoyed playing Scrabble too. And she liked playing games with a group. The temptation rose up in her to fish some tiles out of the letter bag and join them, but she tamped it down. She didn't want to be involved with Max. She was setting their situation right by not being involved in his visits.

She motioned to the door. "I'll just be getting back to the kitchen."

Her mom didn't even look up as she said, "Okay, honey. That's great."

Max rummaged through the little black bag for new tiles and the clack of it followed her to the door. She paused. Damn it. She loved Scrabble. She wanted to stay.

But she couldn't.

As Max watched her go, an odd tingling took up residence in his stomach. He knew why she was staying away. He'd touched her. Actually he'd forced her to have a reaction to him. Now she didn't feel right being in the same room with him, even though she clearly wanted to play. Her misery was once again his fault.

He hoisted himself from the little plastic chair. "I think I'll go in the kitchen for a glass of water. Can I get anybody anything?"

Various mumbled versions of "No," and "No thanks," sent him on his way out the door.

At the entry to the kitchen, he hesitated. The table was littered with index cards of recipes, but she stood by the window, staring out, looking lost and alone. He stepped in, walked to the refrigerator.

"Just getting a glass of juice."

She spun to face him. "Great. Fine."

He'd already said he was sorry. And pointing out to her that she could join them in the family room sort of felt like pointing out that she was miserable.

He got a glass, poured some juice and hovered, not sure what to say or do. Then he remembered the following Tuesday was Trisha's birthday. Kate had said something about a party, which he assumed meant a gaggle of little girls trying to fit into this small house. And he finally saw a way to make things up to her. A way she could accept. A way that wouldn't look as though he was currying favor.

"I've been thinking."

She didn't look at him. Pretending a sudden interest in the recipe cards, she sat at the table and said, "Oh?"

"Yeah. Trisha's birthday is in a few days and I have that big house and pool...and a housekeeper. I thought it might save you and your mom some work if we had the party at my house."

Her gaze ambled over to his. "That would save us some work."

"And the kids would have a pool to swim in."

"Yeah."

"And a housekeeper to straighten up after."

Her smile turned wistful. "Yeah."

"So why don't we just change the party to Sunday afternoon and invite everyone to my house?"

"Invitations are already out."

"Give me a list and I'll have Annette call everyone."

She licked her lips. His heart stalled. Not from attraction. From hope. He might be attracted to her, but that was pointless. Being her friend, getting along, wasn't. He just wanted to get along. He didn't want to hurt her anymore. And he certainly didn't want to be the cause of her misery.

"Okay."

Her response relieved him so much he almost dropped his juice. "Okay. Great. I'll have Annette set that up." He started for the door, but paused and faced her again. "Why don't you come in and play Scrabble with us?"

Her eyes rose from the recipes until they met his gaze.

"I know I did a stupid thing the other day and I'm sorry. But it almost seems like you're punishing yourself by staying in here."

"Max, we're not supposed to become—whatever it is we're close to becoming."

"You mean friends?"

"Yeah. That's as good a word as any."

"Why not?"

"Because we don't like each other."

"We still have to deal with each other."

"Yeah."

"And for that we should get along."

"I guess."

He smiled, ambled over. "So, let's try the friend route. I swear. No more passes. No more touching." He softened his voice. "We can do this."

She sucked in a breath.

"Come on, Kate. You're in a catch-22. You don't want me alone with Trisha. And in this small house it's harder than hell for us to avoid each other. The only other option is to try to get along."

She hesitated a second, but eventually she said, "Okay."

"Okay."

He left the room without another word, but Kate didn't care. She was having trouble dealing with him because her overwhelming physical attraction had unexpectedly turned emotional on her. She wasn't in love. No. She was yearning to be in love.

Yearning. Not wishing. Not hoping. Yearning.

It made getting along a scary proposition.

But what choice did she have?

Because Trisha only knew eight little girls, the children of her grandparents' neighbors, changing the party to Sunday afternoon at Max's house was an easy fix.

On the day of the party, Max stood in his kitchen, listening to Kate give orders like a general marshalling her troops. After assigning Mrs. Gentry to the fruit, vegetable and cheese tray and her mom to patio decorations, she turned to him.

Wearing a lacy bathing suit cover-up over a green bathing

suit the same color as the one she'd worn the day they'd met, she pointed at him. "You are the lifeguard."

Though he was already dressed for it in his navy blue trunks, the thought of eight screaming elementary school girls yanking on his arms caused him to gape at her. "Me?"

"Your house. Your pool. Your idea."

"Okay. But I haven't been to a kids' party in a while, so I might need a few minutes to adjust."

She turned and smiled at him, and it felt as if his chest exploded. It was only a friendly smile, but it propelled him back in time to the beginning of their marriage when they did things for each other. Loved each other.

"You'll be fine." She glanced down at her list again. After checking off another item, she pivoted away from the kitchen island and walked through the family room, heading for the patio. "Mom? How are those decorations coming?"

He tried not to make too much of that smile. Kate was only abiding by their decision to get along. He'd asked her to do that, but it still amazed him.

Mrs. Gentry, his fifty-something housekeeper who dyed her gray hair red and still liked to wear denim miniskirts, sidled up to him. "Interesting."

He glanced down at her. "What?"

"The way you two get along. It's hard not to be impressed." She peered up at him. "You must have already had the blowout about your past."

They had. Though it hadn't been as much of a blowout as he deserved, Kate had said her piece. And he'd felt awful. Theoretically that was all that needed to be done. "We did. And the other day we talked about becoming friends. That's all that's going on here. Nothing 'interesting.' She wants to make things work for Trisha."

Mrs. Gentry looked up at him, over the rim of her glasses. "You think she's doing this for Trisha?"

"Yes."

"Interesting."

He glared down at her. "Will you stop saying that?"

She moved back to the counter by the sink where she'd been arranging the cheese, fruit and veggie tray. "Why?"

"Because…" He squeezed his eyes shut. "Because I don't know what the hell you mean and it makes me nervous because I know you have good intuition about people."

"It means that her behavior is interesting."

"No, it's not. You're seeing things that aren't there because you don't know the whole story. The new Kate doesn't want me. She's too smart."

"New Kate?"

He shrugged. "She's very different from the woman I married."

"Hum."

He groaned. "Now what?"

"You're very different from the man she married, too. Maybe the two of you should stop thinking about the past, and just look to the future?"

He shook his head and walked away. But like a frisky puppy, the notion followed him outside, and he wondered what would happen if they did stop thinking about their past and focused on the future. If they didn't have a past, would she be so dead set against being attracted to him?

When he walked up behind her and she swung around as if he'd scared her to death, he smiled repentantly. "Sorry." Past 1. Future 0.

"It's okay," she said, but her eyes darkened and her gaze dipped to his chest before racing back up again.

Mini fireworks exploded inside him. She might think being attracted was wrong, but she was still attracted. Maybe hope wasn't a zero after all? He squelched that thought. Damn Mrs.

Gentry for filling his head with nonsense. He'd seen Kate's reaction to him touching her. She'd gotten angry—

Actually, she'd gotten angry after her eyes had drifted shut with something that looked very much like longing.

Oh, damn. He had to stop this! Kate wanted nothing to do with him. He couldn't let Mrs. Gentry's optimism fill him with hope for something that couldn't be. Especially not on an afternoon that promised to be trying at best, with Kate's dad relegated to a chair on the patio and her mom flying around pretending she wasn't nervous having her husband out of the house. Add to that the prospect of a patio filled with eight screaming seven-year-olds, and he had to get his brain in the game.

The first child arrived. Wearing a bathing suit with a cartoon character on the front and carrying a huge gift, Bethany Martin scrambled over to Trisha. "Happy birthday." She handed her the box.

Trisha put it on the outdoor table they'd decorated to hold presents. She turned around just in time to find Samantha Rivers standing behind her. Sam's gift was smaller. Grinning toothlessly, she handed it to Trisha.

Trisha shook it. "Is this clothes for Rachel?"

Sam just continued to grin. But Kate scurried over. "It's not polite to shake your gifts or ask what they are." She turned both Sam and Trisha in the direction of the fruit tray Mrs. G. had brought out. "Have some fruit while we wait for the other kids."

Even as the words came out of her mouth, Ginny Johnson scooted across the blue tile patio. "Hey, Trisha!" She handed Trisha a brightly wrapped box.

Following behind, Ginny's mom, Heather, removed her sunglasses. "Hey, Kate, Bev, Dennis…" She let her gaze wander over to Max. "Max. Thanks for inviting Ginny."

Max expected Kate to say something. When she didn't—

only studied Heather with narrowed eyes—he quickly said, "It's our pleasure."

Kate just continued to stare at Heather as she walked over to Max. Wearing white short-shorts and an airy top, Ginny's mom displayed a deep, rich tan. Gold bangle bracelets jingled as she walked. She chewed the tip of the stem of her white sunglasses. "Thanks." Her voice was soft and breathy, as her gaze unabashedly roamed all over Max.

Before he had a chance to register how uncomfortable that made him, Kate slipped beside Heather and slid her arm beneath hers, turning her around. "Thanks for bringing Ginny." She began walking her to the door in the fence that would take Heather to the front yard and eventually the driveway. "I'm sure she'll have a great time. Party's over at four." She opened the gate and all but shoved Heather out. "We'll see you then."

With that she closed the door and faced the pool. Though the kids were now screeching happily at the prospect of an afternoon of swimming and Bev and Dennis were occupied, Mrs. G. and Max stared at her. She was jealous!

Her face red, she walked over to the pool, scooping up kids' cover-ups where they'd dropped them in anticipation of jumping into the water.

He walked over to her. "You okay?"

She looked up with a smile. "Fine. Why?"

"You all but booted Heather Johnson out of the pool area and now you're behaving as if nothing happened."

"I didn't boot her." She scooped up a few more cover-ups. "I just don't want to encourage parents to stay and crowd the place."

She wouldn't look at him while she spoke. A sure indicator with Kate that she didn't want to talk about whatever he'd brought up.

Three more kids arrived. She happily directed them to the

gift table and their parents out the door, as if that had been her intended plan. But Max stared at her with narrowed eyes.

She'd been jealous. She might think she'd covered it, but he was not fooled. If she was jealous that meant she was still attracted—maybe even that she cared for him.

Delicious, heart-stopping hope flooded him as the clap of her hands brought everybody's attention to her.

"Okay. Everybody's here so you guys can start swimming." She pointed at Max. "Trisha's dad is lifeguard. So everybody promise me right now that you'll listen to him."

Eight little heads bobbed in agreement. The sun seemed to make the colors of their suits even brighter. The blue sky swirled peacefully overhead. A breeze rustled through the azalea bushes along the fenceline.

Kate sucked in a breath and said, "Great." Then she turned and headed to the house. Head high, overbright smile on her face, she marched away, opened the French door and slipped inside.

Max couldn't help it. He laughed. The oddest guffaw erupted from him. She liked him and she couldn't hide it.

The girls swam for twenty minutes. Most proved themselves to be excellent swimmers. Max took a seat on the edge of an available chaise lounge, letting his whistle dangle between his knees. The girls screamed and screeched as they landed in the water, or hoisted themselves out of the pool or scrambled to the diving board.

Peace settled over him. He was happy watching Trisha and her friends. It felt right, good, to be a dad. Not just a dad but an active dad. He couldn't have done this eight years ago. But he was doing it now. Happily. Easily.

With the hope caused by Kate's jealousy still in his blood, he couldn't help wondering if this was what would it be like if he and Kate got back together—

He stopped his thoughts. It was one thing to realize what

he'd lost. To wish things were different. But face-to-face with the knowledge that Kate still had feelings for him, the idea of reconciling wasn't abstract anymore. He could woo her. He could get her back.

His heart froze in his chest. His breathing became jerky. It was the worst idea he'd had in years. He was different, but she was different too. Very different. Good Lord, he couldn't count the times she'd stood up to him. Stood her ground. Hell, she'd left Pine Ward and had a job. With nothing but her wits, she'd left him and made a home for herself and their daughter. She was a project manager for a development company similar to Montgomery Development. She could probably give him tips.

If they wanted to get back together, it would have to be on new terms.

As two different people.

Starting over.

He ran his hand across his jaw. Starting over? With a wife and a kid? Right now his life ran smoothly. Marriage would be a complication. Living with Trisha would add stress. And stress had once driven him so far into the bottle he worried he wouldn't get out. Worse, he wasn't even sure he liked the new Kate. He wasn't sure everything he felt for her wasn't just leftover feelings from the happy part of their marriage.

Dennis ambled over. "You okay, boy?"

The expression on his face must have been a sight for Dennis to have noticed. Still, there was no way he'd tell his former father-in-law why. "Hey, you've been sprung from the chair!"

Dennis laughed and settled on the chaise beside Max. "I'm swapping one chair for another."

Bev dropped a pillow behind his head. "It's good for him to get some sun."

Max glanced at Dennis who shrugged as if to say there

was nothing he could do about his overly protective wife. Max smiled weakly at Bev. Not knowing what else to say, he said, "Sun is good."

With a long breath, Bev took the chaise beside Dennis's. Max looked out over the pool, making sure everyone was okay. With eight heads bobbing in the water as they played a game of slap the ball back and forth, he glanced at Dennis again.

Dennis's eyes narrowed, then he smiled. "You know, with me and Bev here poolside, if you wanted to start setting up the grill for those hot dogs, we could watch the girls."

Bev gasped. "You can't be lifeguard!"

Easy as pie, Dennis said, "I can't. But you can."

"I…I…"

Knowing Dennis was ditching his wife and not wanting to be in the middle of this, Max said nothing.

Dennis waved his hand. "My wife is Red Cross certified. Redoes her certification every year. She could be a lifeguard for lifeguards." He shooed Max away. "We're fine."

Max cast a wary glance at Bev, who looked at Dennis.

He motioned to his chair. "For Pete's sake. I'm not going anywhere." He glanced at Bev. "And you could use a minute doing something you love."

She wiggled on the chair as if eager to watch the girls. "I could."

Max rose. "Great. Then I'll start the grill."

Bev stood up, surveyed the pool area. "Okay."

Max handed his whistle to her. As he walked away, he saw Dennis ease down to get more comfortable on his chaise. His eyes happily followed his wife, and Max shook his head. They loved each other and knew each other well enough that Dennis had finally figured out how to eke out a little peace and privacy without hurting his wife.

They might be a tad crazy, but who wasn't? And in the

end, they were cute in the way they were good to each other. He and Kate had had a totally different kind of marriage. They were either totally nuts about each other, falling all over themselves to please each other—or they were fighting.

Something else to remember the next time he thought about wooing her.

He stepped into the family room and headed into the kitchen. "Where are the hot dogs?"

Kate glanced up with a gasp. "Who's watching the kids?"

"Your mom."

Her eyes widened. "Who's watching Dad?"

He smiled wickedly. "No one. I think that was his plan."

Kate's face fell. "Oh, that's not good."

"They're fine." He peeked over at her. She looked adorable in her lacy cover-up over a green bikini, with her pretty hair in a ponytail. Instinctively, his attraction sprang up, stealing his breath. In spite of all the good rational thoughts he'd had about why they shouldn't even consider reconciling, the urge was strong to tease her about being jealous, to step close, to tempt her into admitting she wanted him.

But when he thought about what a bad husband he'd been, about how he didn't really know "this" Kate, about how shaky his own control was, he stopped himself. He didn't want to hurt her again, no more than he wanted to get hurt again himself.

Maybe she'd been right to pretend she hadn't been jealous, that she didn't feel anything, that she didn't want to feel anything.

He glanced around. "So where are the hot dogs and hamburgers?"

She scrambled to the other side of the room, as far away from him as she could get, once again confirming that she wanted nothing to do with him. Unfortunately, she stopped right beside the spice cabinet. The cabinet he needed to rifle through to find the hamburger seasoning.

"Probably in the fridge." She turned and quickly said, "Don't you have to let the grill heat before you can cook them?"

Trying to be non-threatening, he walked over. "It's gas."

Kate's heart kicked against her ribs. He could have told her that from across the room, but she knew why he was following her. She'd been jealous and he'd seen. And now he would try something stupid, like making a pass that she'd have to rebuff.

He reached around her and opened a cupboard door. His arm brushed her shoulder and through the thin material of her cover-up, she swore she could feel his skin. But when he grabbed the seasoning for the hamburger, her heart slowed. He'd actually had a good reason to come over. Then his arm floated across her line of vision. And so did the corner of his chest.

He was close enough to touch.

Her heart kicked up again. The attraction she'd always felt to him slammed through her like a tsunami. Damn him! How could she be attracted to him when the end of their marriage had been so miserable? She knew, the whole way to her soul, that she did not want to get involved with him again. So why did she find him damned near irresistible?

Who knew? The point was she did find him damned near irresistible. It might be confusing, but she was strong. She could handle anything he did. Now that they were close and she was breathing shallowly, he'd undoubtedly take advantage.

She mentally prepared herself to rebuff him as, spice in hand, he faced her. But instead of stepping close or even catching her gaze, he pulled away from her.

Strolling to the refrigerator, he said, "The girls are having a great time. You should go outside and watch them. It's fun."

She frowned. He was giving her an out? Where was the teasing, the tempting, the flirting? "You want me to leave?"

"I want us to keep this party moving."

Still confused, she watched with narrowed eyes as he puttered around the kitchen. "Which means I have to stay inside. I still have some prep work to do."

He walked back to the refrigerator. "Okay."

It wasn't the okay, but the way he said it that sent chills down her spine. It was so neutral, so indifferent that it didn't remind her of something he'd done in the past. No. The old Max was a charmer, a sweet-talker. This guy was so casual that she was beginning to feel foolish for being so sure he'd take advantage of her.

And that scared her. Made her breath shiver and her muscles tense. It was like being attracted to a different guy, so the old rules, the old problems, the old issues from their marriage didn't count.

And that scared her even more.

The hand she held hovering over a bag of potato chips drooped. The issues from their marriage didn't count? What the hell was happening here?

She spun to face him. "You know what? The prep can wait. I think I will go see the girls."

Not waiting for a reply, she raced outside. Oppressive heat hit her immediately, making her feel even more lightheaded than she was. How could she ever, even for one minute think the old issues of their marriage didn't count? She combed her fingers through her hair. Was she crazy?

She had to be. Only a fool would be attracted to a guy who had hurt her so much.

She had to remember their marriage. Remember the nights she'd spent alone. Remember the broken promises. Remember her parents' broken vase. Remember his anger. His lack of control. His lies.

By the time he brought the hot dogs to the grill, she was fortified enough that she could scoop up the bags of buns and take them to the table beside him. As he stood watching the hot dogs and hamburgers, she maneuvered around him without even once worrying that her attraction would rear up. Her very vivid memories would not let it.

When the party was over, they gathered the containers of leftover food and he helped her load them into her car. She appreciated that, but absolutely wouldn't let her guard down. Then he buckled Trisha into her car seat and brushed a quick kiss across her forehead. Something he hadn't done before.

Her chest involuntarily tightened at the sweetness of it, and then melted when Trisha looked up at him with a loving smile.

Her baby loved her daddy.

Tears pooled behind her eyelids. Max rounded the hood, stood beside her and leaned in to whisper, "Did you see that?"

Her first reaction was to say something smart, a clever rebuff that would get him away from her. Then the scent of him wafted to her and her eyes felt like drifting closed. Sweet longing swept through her. Not for what they could have had, but for something else. Something foreign. Something she couldn't quite put her finger on. Something that had to be wrong.

So she fought the feeling, took a step back, opened her car door.

"I'll see you…" she paused. They hadn't actually set up a time for him to visit so she didn't know what to say.

Wrapping his hands around the top of her car door, he casually said, "Tomorrow."

She looked up, caught his gaze. His blue eyes shone with happiness. He loved his daughter. And she suddenly recognized the feeling in her gut. The entire time they were married, she'd longed to see that expression on his face. When they'd first gotten married, she'd known he would make a wonderful dad.

Now he did.

But it was too late.

Not too late for Trisha, but too late for her to enjoy the feeling of a wife exploding with sweet emotion for a husband who loved their child.

She pulled back to get into the car, but he caught her hand. "Thank you for this."

She forced her eyes to meet his. "For the party?"

"For letting me be a part of everything."

"I do it for Trisha."

"Well, since I benefit too, I want to thank you."

She stared into his eyes. It would be so easy to pretend they didn't have a past, so easy to pretend that they equally loved their child, so easy to enjoy this moment.

But they did have a past. She'd been burned a million times by this guy. She shouldn't have trouble remembering that.

She pulled her hand away from his. "We'll see you tomorrow."

He stepped back, let her close the door. Once again, she was struck by the fact that he never argued with her, never tried to persuade her to do things she didn't want to do.

Sliding behind the steering wheel, she shook her head. What difference did it make? They were over. Finished. They had a past too awful to forget.

Or forgive.

CHAPTER EIGHT

"IT WAS THE BEST time ever."

Pouring cold cereal into a bowl for Trisha, Kate laughed at her daughter's description of her birthday party. "It looked very much like the best time ever."

"Can we do it again?"

Only half listening, Kate said, "What? Have another party?"

"Have my friends come to Daddy's to swim."

Pulling milk from the refrigerator, Kate remembered her feelings from the night before. The tightness in her chest over the sweetness of Max's feelings for Trisha and Trisha's feelings for him. But the reminder of their bad marriage had brought the balance back. And it always would. There was no way she'd ever want to get involved with Max Montgomery again. She didn't have to worry about being attracted to him. He could be the best-looking, nicest guy in the world and she would resist him.

And Max clearly enjoyed being a hands-on dad. If he wanted to see Trisha and be a part of the real dad experience, maybe it was time they introduced him to playdates? Besides, having lots of kids around was much better than being alone with each other and Trisha.

"A playdate at the pool might be a good idea. But we'll have to ask him."

Kate's mom strolled into the kitchen. "Ask who what?"

"I want my friends to come to Dad's pool."

"Your friends were at your dad's pool yesterday."

Trisha grinned. "We liked it."

Kate's mom laughed, really laughed, for the first time since her husband's stroke.

"You sound better this morning."

"I feel better." Bev crossed to the coffeepot. "We had a good time yesterday."

Even as she said the words, Kate's father came into the kitchen, leaning heavily on his walker. "Good morning."

"Dad!"

"Grandpa!"

He took a seat at the table beside Trisha as if it were perfectly normal for him to be there. Bev set a cup of coffee in front of him.

"So where's my oatmeal?"

Trisha gasped as if his request shocked her. Kate laughed. Obviously some kind of compromise had been struck the day before. He was dressed and coming to the kitchen for his breakfast—his wish—and eating oatmeal without complaint, which was her mom's wish.

"Coming right up, Dad."

The meal that followed was probably the happiest Kate and Trisha had spent with her parents since their arrival. When they had finished eating, her dad pushed away from the table and invited Trisha to come into the family room and watch cartoons with him.

She happily slid off her chair and followed him out of the kitchen.

Kate faced her mom. "I don't know what agreement you two came to yesterday, but Dad looks great."

Bev began loading the dishwasher. "Seeing your dad at the pool yesterday, dressed in warm clothes, sitting on a chair while the rest of us were enjoying ourselves, I recognized how foolish I'd been." She sighed. "I was afraid, but dressing him in blue jeans and a work shirt weren't really helping. Neither was forcing him to stay in bed."

"That's great."

"Yes. Melanie—" she said, referring to the therapist "—is going to be thrilled."

Kate laughed just as the phone rang. She walked to the old-fashioned white wall phone near the door and answered. "Hello."

"Hey, Kate. It's me."

Max.

Just hearing his voice caused her chest to tighten, her heart to thrum. But she quickly remembered the night she'd left him and brought herself back to sanity.

"What's up, Max?"

"I'm not going to be able to see Trisha today."

She walked over to the sink as her mom left the room, motioning with her hand that Kate should start the dishwasher when her conversation was over.

"That might be a good thing. She's going to ask you to host a playdate at your pool."

She could hear the wince in his voice as he said, "Is it anything like her birthday party?"

"It's exactly like her birthday party, except without the presents and grilling."

"I suppose we can handle it."

Her eyebrows rose in surprise at how easily he'd accepted that, even though it was clear he didn't want to. "She'll be thrilled."

"Good, because I need to ask a favor."

Of course. He needed a favor. That was why he'd been so accommodating.

"Annette just reminded me that I have a ribbon-cutting on Friday."

Her hand stopped halfway to the faucet. Not just a favor, but a public event. "Oh."

"I know you hate them. But I'd love for Trisha to be there." He paused, then added, "My mom will also be there."

"Oh."

He laughed. "I know you and my mom weren't the best of friends, but she's changed."

"Really?"

"Yes. Without Dad, our lives are very different. Plus, this would be a great time for my mom to meet Trisha."

Old feelings sprang to life. Not the pressure to be perfect or even the hours of smiling when she wanted to run, but the heart squeeze that always accompanied his cajoling. Charming Max. Getting her to do something she didn't want to do.

"But I'll also understand if you don't want to go. I know the social aspect of my job wasn't one of your favorite parts of our marriage. I also recognize it might be better for my mom to meet Trisha under more private circumstances."

She swallowed the lump in her throat. He was backing down? That had to be at least the fourth time he could have cajoled, but he hadn't. And this was the second time he'd given her a way out. "How about if I think about it?"

"We have a few days. And my plans don't have to be set in stone. You can decide the time we leave—as long as we get there by two."

"Where's there?"

"North Point."

"New York?"

"Yes."

"So we'll be flying?"

"Yes." He paused. "Look, maybe this was a bad idea. Maybe what we should do is forget about the ribbon-cutting and set up a swim time for Saturday. You call the kids and I'll invite my mom. That way Trisha can meet her second grandma in a less stressful environment."

"And have her miss seeing her dad cut a ribbon on a building he built?" It was one of those damned-if-you-do, damned-if-you-don't situations. She wanted Trisha to know her dad, everything about him and be proud of him, but her memories of that part of their life were hideous.

"Actually, I was hoping Trisha could cut the ribbon."

She squeezed her eyes shut. Trisha would squeal with delight over that. Her mom might be a skittish publicity hater, but Trisha lived for attention.

"She'd love that."

After a few seconds of quiet, Max said, "You know she's my only heir."

"I suspected as much."

"With Chance out of the picture, someday the company will be hers."

"You're not planning on having any other kids?"

He laughed. "I'm forty-two and I already told you I haven't had a real love interest in my life since you."

Her heart stumbled at that. Yes, he had told her that. But then he'd touched her and she'd melted and then gotten angry and sort of forgotten that he'd said it.

"I think the odds are Trisha will be an only child. And though seven's a bit young to be learning about the family business, I don't think she's too young to begin seeing her roots, the people she comes from."

Neither did Kate. She'd had seven years of having Trisha to herself. Seven years of being away from Max and his very public life. If he could be patient and accommodating, then she should be too.

"Okay. We'll go. What time do we need to be at the airstrip?"

"If you get there at eleven, we can have lunch on the plane."

"Sounds good."

"Okay. We'll see you then."

Kate hung up the phone, but paused before going to the dishwasher. Trisha might enjoy the ribbon-cutting festivities, but Kate's stomach plummeted. Still, she didn't have to be part of the ceremony. She didn't have to pose for pictures. She didn't have to talk to the press. She simply had to figure out how to stay out of the limelight without looking obvious.

In the end, she dressed in jeans and a T-shirt. New jeans and a good T-shirt, but informal clothes all the same. Clothes that would quickly tell Max that she hadn't come to be a part of things. Conversely, she dressed Trisha in a pretty pink sundress and put her sable-colored locks in two fat pigtails adorned with big pink bows. Sunday best. Clothes that would look good in photographs.

They arrived at the airstrip at exactly eleven, just in time to see Max's mom, Gwen, climbing out of a black limo. Wearing a slim black pantsuit that accented her perfectly coiffed white hair and still-trim figure, Gwen was the picture of a wealthy family matriarch.

She sucked in a breath and turned to Trisha. "That's Daddy's mom. Your other grandma."

Trisha glanced at the limo. "Her hair is white."

Kate opened her car door. "She's not like my mom. She doesn't dye her hair."

Outside in the hot August sun, she opened the door to the backseat and helped Trisha out. A slight breeze blew dust across the tarmac. A bigger-than-she'd-expected blue jet sat at the ready, entrance open and rolling stairway awaiting them.

She drew in a fortifying breath. "Let's go."

As they walked in the direction of the jet, Max slid his arm across his mother's shoulders and turned her to face them. She couldn't hear what he said, but from the smile that came to Gwen's lips, she guessed he'd told her the pretty little girl in pink was her granddaughter.

She walked over to meet them. "So this is Trisha."

"Hi, other grandma."

Gwen pressed her hand to her chest and laughed. "Isn't that sweet!" She caught Kate's gaze. "She's adorable."

"Thanks. But I think Max's good genes had a lot to do with that."

Gwen laughed again as she stooped down to take in the little girl before her. "You are precious."

Trish grinned toothlessly.

"And toothless!" She tweaked her cheek. "I hope the tooth fairy paid you handsomely for those two teeth."

"Twenty bucks," Trish proudly announced.

"Good." Gwen rose and caught Trisha's hand. "Because front teeth are always worth more."

With that they walked toward the stairway leading into the plane, Kate following a few steps behind them. They stopped in front of Max who reached down and hoisted Trisha up into his arms. "You're all dressed up."

"So are you."

"Nah. Daddy wears suits all the time. Do you know where we're going?"

She nodded and pointed behind her. "In a plane."

"We're going to New York to officially open a building Daddy's company built. If you're good, we're going to let you cut the ribbon."

Not as impressed as she should have been, Trisha shrugged.

Max laughed. "I think I'm learning a very important lesson about parenting. Kids keep you humble."

"Oh, they definitely do," Gwen said and started over to the steps. "Come on, little one. You and I are going to think of a better name for me than other grandma."

Trisha slid down and scampered to her grandmother.

Max faced Kate. "Thanks for bringing her. We'll be back around eight."

Her heart about leaped out of her chest. He thought she was only dropping Trisha off? "Our deal was that you don't see Trisha without me present. I'm coming with you."

"Oh!" His face reddened. "Oh. Great. Really. I just thought—" He pointed at her T-shirt and jeans.

"I'll be in the background. Nobody even needs to know who I am."

Guilt slashed through him. He remembered her absolute hatred of the public appearances they'd had to do as a married couple, but then he realized that it might not have been the public appearances she hated as much as the "Montgomery happy family appearances." He didn't blame her. If she'd thought pretending to be a happy wife was hard, she should have tried being the "blessed" son of a guy who'd done more to tear their family apart than bring it together. Dressing the way she had might as well have been a neon sign that she didn't want to participate.

Which was fine.

"You look great." He let his gaze fall to her jeans and T-shirt and realized she did look great. Girl-next-door pretty. "Annette will be in the audience. You can sit with her."

Relief flitted across her delicate features. Her lips bowed upward. "You didn't make that poor girl drive the whole way to New York this morning?"

"Nope." Grateful that she'd changed the subject, he slid his arm across her shoulders and directed her to the steps. "She and a boatload of staff took another plane yesterday morning. They set up and made all the necessary connections with the local officials. She'll be eager for the chance to sit in the stands and let somebody else take over."

Halfway up the stairs, Kate laughed. "It will be nice to see her."

The sound of her laughter resonated through him. For the first time ever, she seemed comfortable going to one of their family affairs. Of course, she wouldn't be in front of the cameras. And she wouldn't be Mrs. Maxwell Montgomery.

Two important points to remember.

The plane took off and Max directed everyone to the dining room. Trisha might not have been impressed with the idea of a ribbon-cutting, but the huge decked-out plane—with an office that doubled as a dining room and a sitting area that looked more like a living room—was an entirely different story. By the time they reached their destination, she was sitting in the copilot's seat, wearing his hat.

They entered the waiting limo laughing. Trisha had decided her "other grandma" would be Gi Gi, and, since that sounded French, his mother loved it. They arrived an hour before the event. Time enough for Max to give his ex-wife and daughter a tour of the building and meet with the government officials participating in the ceremony. Ten minutes before the speeches and photo ops were to begin, Kate haltingly backed away from Trisha, Max and his mom.

He could see from the expression on her face that she didn't feel right leaving them and it saddened him to realize she was uncomfortable leaving Trisha with him.

Annette, a short plump brunette, took Kate's elbow and gave a light tug. "Come on. She'll be fine. We don't want to miss getting a good seat."

Kate took a step then paused. Max slid Trisha's hand into his mom's and walked over to her. "Go save a place," he said to Annette who smiled slightly and walked away.

"I'm not going to hurt her."

She looked down at her shoes. "I know."

She said it easily, quickly, totally changing the direction of his thoughts. He was sure he'd have to argue this out.

Instead, the ease with which she answered him all but said she trusted him.

Trusted him.

"I'm not going to steal her."

The absurdity of that made her laugh. Which was exactly what he wanted her to do.

He smiled. "Good."

"I'm fine, really. I just—" She caught his gaze. "You do realize that I rarely leave her?"

It wasn't the first time he'd recognized he was dealing with a different person, but it was the first time he noticed how easily they could talk to each other. No yelling. No fighting. No threats. Just honesty.

"I thought you traveled for your job."

"Not a lot. And when I do she stays with friends." She made a strangled sound. "All right. The few times I've traveled, Mom and Dad came out to Tennessee and stayed with her."

He chuckled. "So this is more about your inability to let go than about her being with me."

She shrugged.

He caught her chin and lifted her face. When her pretty green eyes met his, his heart tripped in his chest. He suddenly realized how much this older, wiser, more mature Kate had bent, compromised, given up in the past few weeks to make sure he had a relationship with their daughter. Gratitude swelled in him. All these weeks he'd been taking. It was time to pay that back.

"I'm going to make this work."

She studied his face for a second, then smiled ruefully. "Look at me. I'm turning all crazy mother on you."

"You're a loving mother. Of my child." The words sang through him, flooding his heart with an emotion so strong he couldn't even name it. "I appreciate that."

She blew out a breath, turned and walked down the hall. Out of sight.

He watched her walk away, filled with something that was part pride and part awe. She might not have been the person at fault in their marriage, but she had been young. Too young to handle their problems. This Kate was mature. Strong. Smart. Wonderful.

He would remember to his dying day that he owed her for the way she so easily integrated Trisha into his life.

And he would probably struggle with his attraction to her every bit as long.

Kate easily found Annette in the back. Out of camera range.

She cringed. Max had probably told his assistant that she hated these family things. Though she appreciated being out of the spotlight, adding that to her fears about leaving Trisha with Max and his mom, she suddenly felt that she was the crazy one. And that was just plain wrong.

Wasn't it?

Max and his family had always been the ones who were just slightly off center. Not her. She'd been the sane one.

Yet his mom hadn't said an angry word about her keeping Trisha away from them. And Max was now making promises. Promises she genuinely believed he intended to keep.

She slid onto the folding chair beside Annette. "Thanks."

Annette smiled. "You're welcome."

That was all they got to say before the speeches started. Grateful for the new office complex with a mini-mall in the lobby, the mayor gave a short talk that glowed with praise and gratitude to the Montgomerys for building in his town.

The vice president of operations for Montgomery Development spoke for ten minutes about great things that were about to happen for the city. And then Max rose. He talked for ten minutes about the great people of North Point, then motioned for his mother and Trisha to join him at the podium. Lifting Trisha into his arms, he introduced her as his daughter and talked about her taking over one day.

Trisha grinned toothlessly and giggled.

The crowd loved her.

"She is adorable," Annette whispered in her ear.

Kate smiled. "Good genes."

"Max is thrilled to be a dad."

She could see that. But she could also see that he wasn't a bit nervous behind the podium. He wasn't angry or disgruntled to be a part of the huge company he considered to be the result of his father's tricks and lies.

Still holding Trisha, he turned and walked to the thick red ribbon strung across the wide glass-door opening for Montgomery Towers. He slid Trisha down and accepted the oversize scissors to cut the ribbon. Carefully wrapping Trisha's hands around the handles, he posed them both for a picture and snapped the scissors closed, cutting the ribbon.

The crowd laughed and applauded.

Kate faced Annette. "How long's he been like this?"

"Like what?"

"Not angry."

Annette's brow furrowed as if she wouldn't talk about her boss, but after a few seconds, her face softened and she sighed. "It started a few months before he quit drinking. At first, I thought he was just trying to keep busy because he missed you. Then I thought maybe he was resigned to the fact that his dad was no great shakes as a father. But then he got interested in the business and I realized he intended to set things right."

She glanced at Annette. "Set things right?"

"Undo the things his dad had done. Or at least not let his dad operate in his usual shady way. He started by doing all union negotiations. Then he moved to reviewing contracts with subcontractors and vendors. Then he began looking at the leases."

As Annette spoke, Kate watched Max posing for the cameras, sometimes holding Trisha, sometimes not. His smiles were genuine. His remarks to the press as they shot questions at him were easy but deliberate. He wasn't a pushover or a sap. He wasn't a figurehead. He wasn't the favorite son destined to inherit the family business. He knew what he was doing.

"All that before he quit drinking?"

"It was almost as if he had to see what he was getting himself into before he could join Alcoholics Anonymous."

"So he changed the company. He didn't adapt."

"Honestly?" Annette said, once again facing her. "I think he grew up."

Kate's gaze crept over to Max again. The man holding her child. The father of her child. And for a split second it was as if she were looking at somebody else. A man she didn't know.

It was crazy.

Yet she couldn't shake the feeling. Especially when a reporter asked about Trisha—why no one had ever met his daughter before. He answered with the simple explanation that he didn't believe it was wrong to keep his daughter out of the public eye until she was ready. He hadn't placed blame. He hadn't gotten embarrassed. He hadn't gotten angry. He hadn't lied.

He'd simply answered.

She stared at him. Really studied him. Unable to comprehend what she was putting together after only a few weeks of being in his company again.

He wasn't the same guy.

Physically he was still the same ruggedly handsome, sexy Max. Emotionally, he was a totally different guy. A smart worker. A hard worker. A man who wanted to be a good dad. A man who no longer cast blame and held grudges.

A good man.

After only a few minutes of questions and pictures, Trisha got antsy. Gwen scooped up her hand, then caught Kate's gaze and nudged her head in the direction of the building, indicating that Kate should come back into Montgomery Towers with them.

Annette more or less bulldozed through the crowd in front of her to get them through, but when she entered the building lobby Gwen passed Trisha's hand to her. "Please take Trisha up to the Montgomery offices on the top floor."

Annette didn't hesitate. This woman was, after all, the owner of the company for which she worked.

But as the elevator door closed behind them, Kate suddenly realized she and her ex-mother-in-law were alone. Completely alone in a barely furnished room that echoed with quiet.

"My son may have forgiven you. I have not."

Kate's limbs froze with fear. She faced Gwen. With her cheeks puffed out and red with rage, the woman was exactly the opposite of the sweet woman who'd met Trisha that morning and more like the woman Kate had known. The one who'd been reconciled to the fact that she'd married the wrong man and determined to make the best of it—for the sake of her sons. Could she expect her to be anything but angry that Kate had hurt one of them?

"He quit drinking no more than nine months after you left. You couldn't have stayed one more year? Told him about his child? Given him a chance?"

"I gave him hundreds of chances."

Gwen snorted and paced away. "Our family had been torn apart. Is still torn apart." She pivoted and faced Kate. "Do you know what it's like never to see your own child?"

She swallowed. They were back to this. Always this. "I'm sorry about Chance leaving, but I—"

"But nothing!" Her angry voice reverberated through the

glass lobby. "We took you in! Made you one of us! And you betrayed us."

"I saved myself. Protected my child." She lifted her chin. "I'd do it again."

"Oh, save your pretty speeches. You may need them for court. Max only told me about Trisha yesterday. So I haven't had time to consult a lawyer. But I will." She smiled without a trace of humor. "I will. And then we'll see how much you like never getting to see your child."

CHAPTER NINE

KATE'S FIRST THOUGHT was to run. To take Trisha and go back to Tennessee. To force them to fight her on her turf, not in the county where they played golf with the judges and contributed to all of their reelection campaigns.

But her running days were over. She'd moved to Tennessee, given up her friends, barely seen her parents for the past eight years because she'd been afraid of Max. But right now she wasn't afraid of Max.

The words rippled through her, along with a strange sensation of emotion. She truly wasn't afraid of him. Not even afraid he'd try to manipulate her. And she realized Charming Max, the boy she'd dated, had only turned into Manipulating Max because of alcohol. Without alcohol, he wasn't either Charming Max or Manipulating Max. He was just Max.

The realization should have shocked her but it didn't. She'd been coming to this conclusion for weeks. Trying to reconcile who he was right now with who he had been. But it suddenly struck her that she might be making a mistake thinking of him as old Max and new Max when it was more like she was dealing with a totally different guy.

She would have loved to have had a few days to test out that theory before she confronted him. Unfortunately, she wasn't about to let a threat go unanswered.

By the time she got Trisha home and unwound enough

from the busy day to go to bed, it was after nine. Still, she raced out to her car and made her way to Max's.

The house was dark when she arrived. Wisps of white clouds played peek-a-boo with the moon. A million stars shone overhead. After turning off her ignition, she sat in his driveway for a few seconds, debating going in. Finally she just shoved open the car door and bounded up his front walk.

She rang the bell and after a few minutes, Max answered. Still in his black suit, with the top buttons of his white shirt undone and his red tie loosened, he looked sexily rumpled. Like a guy begging to be seduced by the woman he loves after a hard day at work.

Oh, Lord! Where had that come from?

"Kate?"

She blinked, bringing herself back to the real world. "We need to talk."

He stepped back and opened the door wide enough for her to enter. "We do?"

As she walked into the foyer, he motioned toward the kitchen. "I was just about to get a glass of lemonade."

She followed him, and as he walked to the refrigerator she sat on one of the tall stools by the granite-covered island. "Your mom threatened to take me to court over Trisha this afternoon."

Max stopped midway, spun around and gaped at her. "What?"

"She's seeing a lawyer tomorrow. She didn't precisely say she was going for custody, but she told me to save my apologies and pretty speeches for court. She also told me to prepare to get to know what it feels like never to see your own child."

Max groaned. "You're kidding."

"I wish I were. But she was very clear."

He groaned again, resuming his walk to the fridge. "You have to believe I'm not behind this."

"I do. Actually, that's why I'm here. I won't buckle under threats anymore. If that's how your mom wants to operate, I think it's just plain sad, but I won't play that game."

To her complete surprise, he laughed. "Good for you." He displayed a jug of lemonade. "Can I get you some?"

Relieved that he wasn't just taking this good-naturedly, but also clearly was uninvolved, she licked her dry lips and realized she was parched. She let out the breath that had backed up in her lungs. "Yeah. Thanks."

He brought the glass over to the counter where she sat. As he handed it to her, their fingers brushed, just the slightest bit, but electricity crackled at the contact. Their eyes met, and she quickly looked away.

She'd never dealt with normal, sane, mature Max before. And she liked this Max. Really, dangerously liked this Max.

When he sat on the stool beside hers, the room suddenly felt small and close. Her breath stuttered out of her chest.

He smiled at her. "I'm glad you're here."

Part of her was glad too. He was such a nice guy. So easy to deal with. So sweet. So good to Trisha. So good to her.

The other part of her was—

Wow. The other part was nothing. Her wary self seemed to be gone.

She gulped some lemonade, scrambling to remember the night she'd left so she could regain her perspective. She had to be careful around him. That was how she stayed safe.

"I like that you turned to me."

She swallowed hard. In spite of her wariness, something warm and tingly fluttered through her. She liked being able to turn to him too. Not for rescue, but to hold up his half of the parenting team they made. And there was nothing wrong with that.

She glanced down at her lemonade. "It feels good to be

able to turn to you." Braver now that they were in normal territory, she looked over at him again.

Warmth filled his eyes when he smiled at her. "Thanks."

She hadn't forgotten how good looking he was or how susceptible she was to those good looks, but the zing of attraction that raced through her had a different feel to it. A fresh feel. Like moonlight winking off new snow. It felt bright, new, special.

That was not good.

She cleared her throat. "Anyway. I don't want to fight your mom."

"You won't," he calmly assured her. "Any custody or visitation arrangements will be made by you and me. Only you and me." He sucked in a breath. "Truth be told, I think her anger is actually residual from Chance leaving."

"But that has nothing to do with me."

He sighed heavily, shifted on his stool. "I think having Trisha suddenly in our lives reminds her that we have another missing family member."

"Oh." She'd never even thought of that. "Sorry."

He shook his head. "It's not your fault that Chance is gone or even that my mom's upset. If anything, she knows it's my fault and Dad's. She knows my dad and I had a fight that Chance overheard, but she doesn't know what we were fighting about."

"She still doesn't know Chance is your dad's real son?"

"Nope. I think if she did, it would kill her."

"You almost sound like you're glad Chance stays away."

"Maybe."

"Max." Her voice was soft. Not accusatory. Sympathetic.

He rose from the stool, ran his hand along the back of his neck. "I love him. I miss him. But I'm afraid for my mom." He faced her. "What would happen if he came home? Would he tell her that he overheard me confronting Dad with the rumors I picked up at the office? Would he tell her he knows our dad really was his biological father? Would he tell her that he hates that his life is a sham?" He squeezed his eyes shut in misery. "My mom raised him. As her son. Clueless that he was the product of my dad's adulterous affair, she took him in and kissed him and cuddled him, packed his lunches and took him to Little League. She misses him. Longs for him. But Chance feels it was all a lie. I can't help worrying about what would happen if he came home."

"I'd worry too." But she wasn't concerned for Max's mom. She wasn't even concerned for Chance. She was worried for Max. He'd started drinking after the argument with his dad, the one Chance had overheard. Would he start again if Chance came home?

A shudder worked through her. She didn't want to test that out any more than he did.

"Anyway, I know that's why she confronted you today. She's angry that Chance is gone. She feels he was ripped away from her. She's mixing his situation and our situation together and coming up with feelings that aren't fair."

"As long as we can work it out."

"We can."

"You can speak for your mom?"

He laughed. "Yes. I'll just remind her that we stay in the present. It was the deal we struck right after I quit drinking. We don't think about yesterday. We don't think about tomorrow. We deal in today."

She smiled ruefully. "I sure threw a monkey wrench into that."

He returned to the stool beside her, caught her hand, forcing her to look at him. "That's not how I see it. I see you coming home, introducing me to my child, as a great blessing."

Relief rushed through her, along with a swell of attraction. What she wouldn't give to be able to like this guy. To have a relationship not haunted by the past. "And there isn't even a little part of you that's angry?"

"There was. But I reminded that part of me that you did what you believed you had to do."

"Say it often enough and you convinced yourself?"

He chuckled. "Something like that." He smiled at her again. "But better. I don't want to live in that confusing, painful past. All being angry with you does is bring up a part of my life I wish had never happened. I'd prefer to enjoy the gift."

Her heart twisted a bit. What he said made so much sense. She began to understand why being with him, being attracted to him right now felt so different. This was no charismatic, fun-loving boy with sexy promises in his hot blue eyes. This was a man with promises of honesty and commitment in his deep blue eyes. Promises that were even sexier to a woman who'd been alone for so long.

"So I will talk to my mom tomorrow." He finished his lemonade and rose from his stool. "I will tell her no lawyers. I will remind her that we deal in today."

Disappointment rattled through her. They were done? No more talking? No more closeness?

She rose too. "Thanks."

"You're welcome."

He walked her to the front door and like a ninny, she paused. She felt like a star-struck teenager suddenly alone with the high-school quarterback, knowing nothing could ever come of all the wonderful things she was feeling, but unable to stop feeling them.

She looked up at him with a hesitant smile. He glanced down at her, returning her smile.

And suddenly she realized something amazing. Gazing into his pretty blue eyes, she wasn't thinking of the past. She was thinking only of this Max. She liked him. This guy right here, right now. He wasn't a cajoler. He wasn't sweet-talking her into doing things she didn't want to do. He didn't try to sugarcoat his past. He didn't try to seduce her with words or kiss her into agreeable oblivion. He just—

Kissed her?

His head had descended slowly until his lips were on hers. All the air disappeared from her lungs. Warmth exploded in her middle and speared to all parts of her body. The giddy schoolgirl disappeared, replaced by a woman. A woman oh so hungry for all the things she'd missed out on in the past eight years.

Excitement surged through her, and she returned his kiss, but softly, tentatively. This wasn't the kiss of long-lost lovers. This was a first kiss. Two people getting to know each other. Experimenting with the feel of each other's lips, each other's taste.

As if thinking the thought made it happen, Max coaxed her lips open with a sweep of his tongue and with a groan she complied. His hand slid from beneath her hair to her shoulders to nudge her closer, nestling her breasts against his chest as their tongues twisted and swirled.

Far too quickly, he retreated. Their lips brushed over each other a few more times and then he pulled away.

Mesmerized, her body thrumming with sensations and needs she'd thought long dead, she stepped back. Reaching up, she traced the smooth line of his mouth. He looked the same. Only a little more mature. But he was so different. So different.

He bumped his forehead to hers. "That was amazing."

She squeezed her eyes shut. *I liked the kiss too.* She almost said it. The words sang through her blood, fluttered through her heart.

But her brain knew better. He might behave differently, but at the end of the day he was still Max. Still an alcoholic.

Still the ex-husband who had broken so many promises she couldn't keep track. And if she forgot that, if she let herself get involved with him, or even let herself trust him too much, the real Max would spring up someday and hurt her.

But she wouldn't forget because she was different too. Not the wimpy twenty-something, afraid to stand up to him. She was strong. Smart.

She took another step back, grabbing the doorknob. "I've gotta go."

And with that she left him. She didn't think about the kiss on the way home. Didn't let herself recall all the wonderful sensations or even the way her body came to life with a few sweeps of his tongue. She unlocked the door to her parents' quiet house, tiptoed up the stairway and slid into bed, promising herself she'd never let him kiss her again.

He shouldn't have kissed her. Soaping himself in the shower the next morning, the words rang through Max's brain like a litany of recrimination.

I shouldn't have kissed her.
I shouldn't have kissed her.
I shouldn't have kissed her!

He liked hearing her laugh. He liked making her laugh. He loved parenting with her, and he had jeopardized all that just because he couldn't keep his hands off her. Couldn't stop his fingers from sliding beneath the thick mane of the sable hair at her nape. Feeling its weight, enjoying the feminine softness. He couldn't stop his head from descending, his lips from taking just one taste.

But one taste grew into two, and a kiss that was supposed to be a wisp of a touch grew into something warm and deep and hungry. Every ounce of pent-up longing buried inside him sprang to life, believing it was about to be satisfied.

But it wasn't. Not because he wasn't attracted to her or

even because she wasn't attracted to him. Because it was wrong. She was different than the Kate he'd married.

He frowned. No, she wasn't so much different as changed. She was still herself but spunkier. Also sensible and…well, mature. That was it. Mature. Even if they hadn't divorced, she would have grown into this mature woman. As soon as they had Trisha, she would have become this Mama Bear who wouldn't let anybody hurt her baby. He smiled. Oh, he could just imagine that! Her dictating when and how his dad could see Trisha? That made him laugh as he stepped out of the shower. He would have liked to be sober to see that.

Had he been sober, he would have seen that.

The distance between them was all his fault.

Those were the words ringing in his ears as he drove to his mother's mansion on the hill. He popped the door of his Range Rover and walked up to the main entrance, only to discover Phillip, her butler, was already at the door as if expecting him.

"Your mother's in the dining room, Mr. Montgomery."

He didn't waste a second. His mother should not have interfered. Not only was it not her place, but that kind of behavior would only remind Kate of a very bad time. A time when she'd had to struggle for her life. A time when arguing was better than cooperation. If his mother ruined the good relationship he and Kate were forming, they would all be sorry.

Still, when he stepped into the dining room none of the anger he felt showed on his face. Control over his emotions was second nature now. He didn't have to remind himself that anger solved nothing. He knew anger solved nothing. He also knew how to negotiate. How to take and keep the upper hand when it belonged to him and step away when it didn't.

Walking to the table, he said, "Mother." He crossed to her chair, kissed her cheek and then took his usual seat. "I'm glad I haven't yet eaten breakfast."

"So am I. The pancakes were especially fluffy this morning. You should have those."

He smiled at Cook, who stood beside his chair awaiting his instructions. "Pancakes it is." Opening his napkin, he said, "So what's this I hear about you threatening Kate over Trisha?"

Gwen sighed as if put upon. "I wasn't threatening her, darling. Consulting a lawyer is only common sense."

"No, it isn't. It's interfering. When Kate left eight years ago I was unreliable. Sometimes frightening. Always undependable." He took a sip of coffee. "She left to protect herself and Trisha. If you make her life difficult, you'll be the one to suffer. We'll cut the time you get to spend with your granddaughter and make it so that you don't see her without Kate present, so that you can't interrogate her or poison her mind."

His mother set her hand on top of his with a warm laugh. "Really, darling, such theatrics!"

"You're the one who threatened Kate, Mom."

"I just want our rights protected."

"You do remember Kate, right? Sweet girl. Wouldn't hurt a fly. She'll give us our rights without courtrooms or lawyers or even much of a fuss, if we just play fair."

"She didn't play fair."

"She was afraid."

"There was no reason to be afraid!"

He sighed. "Mom, you didn't live with me. You don't know what she went through. I'm amazed she didn't bolt the second she saw me at the hospital last month. But I'm grateful that she didn't and I'm grateful that she lets me see Trisha and I'm working my way into her good graces so that we can parent together."

His mom's eyes lit with joy. "You're trying to get back together?"

Good Lord. How had she come up with that out of what he'd said?

"No!" But even as he denied it, he remembered that kiss. He remembered how his hand had itched to slide farther down her back, along the slim curve of her waist. He remembered the heat in his blood and the ache in his heart.

But he also remembered that she had evolved. She was different. He was different. As these two people, they might not be a good match. "No."

"I think you should."

"Mom, that isn't even slightly on the cards. If you talk like that around Kate she's going to get nervous and stay away."

"Wow. Can't talk about how she kept my granddaughter from us. Can't talk about a reconciliation." She held up her hands in surrender. "I suppose I just have to shut up completely."

"That would be an excellent idea."

"Seems like she's calling all the shots."

"Or fighting for her life."

His mom harrumphed. "Drama queen."

"Again, Mom, you didn't know what it was like to live with me. We have to play fair. Be honest and open with her so she isn't afraid of dealing with us."

The room got quiet as the words he'd said to his mom sank into his own head and made him realize he wasn't being totally honest. Not with himself. Not with Kate. He'd kissed her because he liked her. He liked the woman she'd become as much, if not more, than the girl he'd married. He knew with every fiber of his being that they would be a good match. A better match than they had been as kids.

But she didn't want him. And every time he was in her presence he liked her more. One simple kiss had blown him away. Even now, he could feel her softness, taste her taste, feel her surrender. He wanted her so much that it was only a matter of time before he started acting on it. He didn't know when. He didn't know how. But one thing was certain. When he wasn't sure he could control himself, he had to come clean, be honest and get help.

He had to talk to Kate.

CHAPTER TEN

A FEW HOURS LATER, Kate sat at a café table on the sidewalk in front of Antonio's Italian Restaurant. Max had called and asked her to meet him. Alone. Somewhere they could talk without worry that Trisha would overhear. Though she'd been perfectly calm while they arranged this meeting, even while driving downtown to the restaurant, the five-minute wait had sent her mind scampering in a million directions.

He'd said he'd wanted to tell her about the discussion with his mom, but he'd also said there was more. Something he needed to tell her. Something Trisha shouldn't overhear.

What if the conversation with his mom hadn't gone well?

What if he wanted joint custody?

What if his mom had convinced him to go to court to block her from taking Trisha back to Tennessee?

Her breath stalled, but Max suddenly appeared. Standing across the street in his jeans and T-shirt, waiting for the light, he looked so different from the lanky boy she'd married.

A shudder of attraction worked its way through her. But with the fearful thoughts she'd just had about him, feeling anything for him was wrong. So she squelched it.

Mercilessly.

It didn't matter if he was gloriously, maturely sexy. It didn't matter that his walk was no longer a boyish swagger, but the stride of a mature man. It didn't matter that his hair fell sexily to his forehead or that his smile, when he noticed her, warmed her heart. It didn't matter that he'd kissed her and she'd enjoyed it and longed for more. There were too many issues between them for her to be attracted to him.

Period.

End of story.

As he sat, she said, "I took the liberty of ordering you an iced tea."

"Thanks. I'm sorry I'm late. I—" He hesitated, nervous.

A waiter in black pants and a white shirt arrived with their teas and when he asked to take their lunch orders, Max relaxed like a man getting a reprieve from death row. But though he relaxed, she got more nervous. If he was happy to delay, whatever he wanted to talk about was not good.

His mom probably had persuaded him to do something. Most likely to try for joint custody. Her nerves hitched another notch.

By the time the waiter left, she thought she'd explode and didn't waste a second. "All right. What's up?"

He chuckled. "Wow. Getting right to it, I see."

"I told you. I'm different."

He looked down at his iced tea. "I know."

She sighed. "Max, I'm not good at waiting for bad news. So just spit it out. Whatever it is I can handle it."

He studied his iced tea for a few more seconds, then slowly raised his gaze until he caught hers. "I think I'm starting to be attracted to you again."

Her heart stopped, then sped up, sending her pulse scrambling. Starting to be attracted? She'd always been attracted to him. And now that he was sober, her feelings had expanded. He was a handsome, sexy, wonderful man. A man she'd slept with. He knew her body as well as she knew his. Knew his likes, his dislikes, the sensitive places—

Oh, God. She got it. He wasn't starting to be attracted to

her. He was only now feeling everything she'd been fighting since the day she'd returned. Except it was harder for him. When he thought of their past, he didn't have the safety net of remembering her breaking windows and shouting. He remembered her scrambling to make things work. Giving him aspirin. Covering for him. Helping him. Maybe even the happiness they'd shared at the beginning of their marriage.

She shifted on her chair. "Max, this is nothing but residuals from…you know…when we were first married."

He laughed. The sound was as warm as the sun and as potent. It struck a chord in her that swelled her heart and sent a shower of tingles down her spine.

"No. It's not residuals from when we were first married."

His confidence kicked her heart rate into overdrive again. How could he say that with so much certainty?

"Kate, you're so damned different that only a fool would think we could go back to what we had. But I also can't lie. There's enough of you that's still the same that sometimes I do tap into old memories and…wonder."

"Wonder?"

He sighed, sat back on his chair. "This morning, thinking about kissing you last night, thinking about how it was the same but different, I realized that at some point—even if we hadn't divorced, you would have grown into this strong woman. You became protective for Trisha. And I'm just about certain you would have put a foot down with my parents." He laughed. "It made me smile to think about it. Because I like this new you. Really, really like this new you."

Her breath shimmied in her chest. She liked the new him too. But it was wrong. They couldn't just wipe away the past. Forget broken windows and anger. Some pains left marks. Scars. Residuals that wouldn't just go away because they wished they would.

"I think that's because the new you fits the new me. We'd

be a killer team. We both have an innate compassion and sense of right and wrong. But we also know ourselves. We're smart. We're strong." He glanced away, then glanced back again with a wince. "I also can't stop myself from wondering how that would play out in bed."

Her heart about popped out of her chest. Her nerves jumped. She could see the two of them naked, exploring, hungry. "Wow. Thanks for that image."

He laughed, then squeezed her hand as if he thought she was teasing and pulled back. "Anyway, I promised myself when I went into AA that I'd never again live a lie. And pretending I feel nothing would only up the tension of an already difficult situation."

"Max—"

"Don't worry. I'm not telling you this to ask you to get back together with me." He looked down at his plate, then back up at her. The hopeful look in his eyes didn't match his next words. "I only want you to know so that you're prepared."

"Okay. I'm prepared." She wasn't. Not even a little bit. As she stared into his hopeful blue eyes, her heart longed to tell him she liked him too. But her brain kept flashing back to pictures of their past. How could she like him so much when he'd hurt her so much?

She took a sip of tea to calm herself, then fluffed out her napkin before laying it across her lap. This seemed like the perfect time to change the subject. "So what happened in your conversation with your mom?"

He sat back. "Everything's settled. I told her that anything to do with Trisha was between us and she should stay out of it."

Ridiculous pride swelled in her chest. He would never have so neatly and cleanly handled his parents eight years ago. Proof, again, that he was a totally different guy.

A totally different guy who was attracted to her—the different person she was, not the girl he'd married.

She sucked in a quiet breath. Temptation and longing surged in her. She ignored both. "And she agreed?"

He smiled ruefully. "I'm her only child now. She can't afford to lose me."

"True."

He reached for his napkin. "So, now that we have both of those things out of the way, what do you say we just enjoy lunch?"

"Sure." But her insides shivered. One word from her could change everything. One sentence. I like the new you too. She'd seen the longing in his eyes. She knew at least a part of him hoped she'd tell him she liked him too.

But once again those damned pictures rolled through her mind, telling her not to think about the effortlessly sexy guy beside her. Not to wonder about how different a marriage to this Maxwell Montgomery would be.

He glanced around. "So what do you think of the updates on this block? They're part of the city's renovation and development program."

"They're great." Nervous, she picked up her tea again. Her hand shook. Seriously. She should leave. Spending too much time with him was tempting fate. "Did you guys have anything to do with them?"

He hesitated for a second, then said, "A bit."

Her eyebrows rose. "A bit?"

He winced. "More than a bit."

Kate took a deep breath. A million questions bombarded her brain, things she wouldn't have been able to ask eight years ago. Not only had she not been as educated in development then as she was now, thanks to her job, but also the old Max had hated his work.

They were both so different.

Longing tugged on her soul and filled her with a weird kind of anger. If she'd just met him, even if he'd told her about his past drinking, she would give him the benefit of the doubt. She'd be nice to him, befriend him, maybe let herself fall hopelessly in love—

But this wasn't their first meeting.

She drew in a silent breath, forcing herself to get back on track. "So tell me about the renovations. How involved were you?"

"I actually poured a lot of my own money into this." He shrugged. "Montgomery Development has so many out-of-town business associates who spend days and sometimes even weeks here, that it's to our benefit to have a hotel or two and a few nice restaurants right here, a few blocks away from our offices. I saw the investment potential and ran with it."

Her eyes widened. "You own this stuff?"

"I own it, but I lease it out." He smiled. "Don't let my money scare you now, Kate. You saw my house. You saw how I live. One housekeeper. And she's around mostly because I can't cook and don't have time to clean. I'm not going to turn into my parents and get a huge house on the hill. I like this lifestyle."

Avoiding his eyes, she rearranged her napkin. "I just thought you stayed in our old house because you hadn't had time to find another place."

"I stayed there because I like the house." He fiddled with his silverware. "I like the house a lot. You did a beautiful job. I'm not surprised you got into construction yourself."

Her gaze swung to his. "You know where I work?"

"I made a few discreet inquiries. Nothing that would raise eyebrows or suspicions. I just wanted to be sure you and Trisha have everything you need."

"I can provide for us."

He laughed. "I know you can. I'm not criticizing. I was

worried, so I checked. And I found that you're doing great."
He paused. "I'm proud of you."

Tears stung her eyes. Emotion clogged her throat. The
old Max wouldn't have noticed what she did. This Max was
proud of her. Oh, he was dangerous to her heart and soul.
Very dangerous. "Thanks."

"You're welcome."

Their food came and the conversation shifted to Trisha.
For which she was eternally grateful. Knowing that he was
starting to have feelings for her, feelings strong enough that
he felt he had to admit them, put a whole new spin on things.
It was dangerous for them to be together. One of them was
bound to slip. And when one slipped, the other would fall.

So now came the hard part. They shouldn't be together.
But if he wanted to see Trisha every day, they'd be seeing
each other a lot.

And the question became: Did she trust him enough to
let him be alone with Trisha? Because there was no way she
could spend any more time with this Max, this new honest Max, without falling hopelessly, head-over-heels in love
with him.

When daddy-visit, playdate day arrived, Max was ready.
Annette had come with her two youngest children. Mrs.
Gentry was in the kitchen making snacks. Stretched out on
a chaise, wearing apricot-colored capris and a white tank
top, was his mom.

He lightly kicked her chaise. "Where's your swimsuit?"

She blinked up at him. "I don't swim. It messes up my
hair."

"You're going to miss all the fun."

"I'm going to watch all the fun."

Just then Annette's two boys raced out of the house and
flew into the pool. Landing with a splash, they drenched

Gwen. She popped off the chaise and turned to yell at them, but suddenly her eyes widened. "Oh, my gosh!"

Worried, Max said, "What?"

"The little one. He looks just like Chance!"

Max followed the direction of her gaze. With yellow hair and big blue eyes, Annette's youngest son did look something like Chance, if only in a very generic, twelve-year-old boy kind of way. So he humored his mom. "Yeah, I guess he does."

"Remember how Chance's hair used to turn almost white in the summer?"

"Mmm-hmm."

She sat on the edge of the chaise, watching the boys swim and bat the beach ball back and forth. "He's cute."

Max took a seat on the chaise beside hers. "All kids are cute, Mom."

She kicked her toe along the tiles beneath the chaise. "You think I'm a silly old fool."

"Never." He smiled at her. Now that she'd butted out of his business with Kate, she was back to being his sort-of-sad, very lonely mom. The mom he wished with every fiber of his being could be happy. Just once in her life. "You simply miss your son."

She snorted a laugh. "Yeah."

He rose from the chaise. "Why don't you just relax and enjoy the afternoon—"

The gate swung open and Trisha ran through.

"—with your granddaughter," he added, hoping she'd take the hint that she should enjoy what she had and forget what she didn't.

Wearing her little blue bathing suit with a ruffle around her hips that made it look like a tutu, Trisha propelled herself at Max's mother.

"Hey, Gi Gi!"

Gwen hugged her. "Hey, yourself. I understand you're having another party."

Trisha's face scrunched. "A playdate. Not a party."

"Oh, excuse me," his mom replied with mock politeness.

Trisha pointed at her grandmother's white tank top. "Where's your suit?"

"I'm not swimming."

Trisha said, "Ah, Gi Gi!"

Kate ambled over. "Yeah, Gi Gi. Where's your sense of fun?"

Max wasn't surprised that Kate had so easily gotten over the incident with his mom threatening to take her to court. He'd handled it and she accepted that he had. But he was surprised when his mom laughed. "Well, I am sort of wet already."

Grateful everybody was getting along, Max grinned. "Might as well get completely wet."

She patted her hair. "It's not like I can't shampoo again at home."

Trisha tugged on her hand. "Come on. We'll ask Mrs. Gentry to find you a suit."

Kate laughed as they walked away. "Only with you for two months and she already knows who to ask for things."

He laughed, his gaze following his daughter until she was inside the French doors, then he turned to Kate. "I don't see your suit anywhere."

She took a step back, looked away. "That's because I'm not swimming. Actually, I was thinking I don't really need to be here."

"You're leaving?"

She shielded her eyes from the sun. "You're fine with her now, Max." Once again she glanced away then looked back at him, as if what she had to say was incredibly difficult for her. "I trust you."

He'd figured that out the day of the ribbon-cutting, but hearing her say it sent pride surging through him. But a wave of disappointment followed on its heels. Kate leaving him alone with their daughter meant he didn't get to spend time with her. And she didn't have to spend time with him. He knew it was for the best, but it still rankled.

"Are you sure you're not going because of what we talked about at the restaurant?"

For Kate, the temptation to lie was strong. Not because it would make the situation easier, but because she didn't want to put any more pressure on Max than he already had. But his honesty at the restaurant had set new ground rules for this relationship and she would abide by them. "That's part of it."

"I understand."

The guilt she heard in his voice shamed her. She couldn't let him take the blame for something that was as much her fault as it was his.

"I don't think you do understand." She looked around again, stalling, hoping for an easy way to say this, then finally gave up and caught his gaze. "I'm not leaving because you told me you liked me. I'm leaving because I like you too."

"Really?" Happy surprise filled his voice.

She quickly added the things he also needed to remember. "Yes. But you know all the reasons it's not wise for us to like each other. You also already said you weren't going to pursue this."

He took a step closer. "I only said that because I thought for sure you didn't even want to consider liking me."

Slowly, cautiously, she caught his gaze. "I don't. I can't." She combed her fingers through her hair. "I shouldn't."

"But—"

"But I can't seem to stop myself."

His expression became so hopeful that her heart hurt.

She shook her head. "Don't! This time if we make a mistake, we don't just hurt us. We hurt Trisha." She sighed heavily. "I won't take that chance."

She turned and walked through the gate, leaving him with his little girl and her friends, trusting him, all because she knew staying would only increase their attraction, maybe push them to the point they'd do something they'd regret.

Kate returned at four, the same time all the other parents were to pick up their kids. Max stood by the pool, looking sexy in his swimming trunks and fatherly in the way he wore his lifeguard whistle and monitored everything going on in the pool.

Her heart melted a bit. He was so gorgeous and so good that not falling for him was sort of like not thinking of the color blue.

Which was wrong. If it killed her, she would keep their relationship platonic. "Hey. I'm here to pick up my daughter."

Spinning to face her, he laughed. "So that's how it is, huh? You're just one of the crowd of parents?"

"Yep." She kept her tone light but even. They might not be able to spend long periods of time together but they could be friendly.

He pointed at a little throng of men who'd gathered by the snack table, waiting for their kids who obviously wanted a few more minutes of play in the pool. Hairy legs and bald heads abounded. "Sure you want to be counted in that group?"

She laughed. "They are our age."

"They're my age. You're six years younger, remember? You're the hot mama. While the rest of us are starting to show signs of wear, you're still as pretty as you ever were."

She tried to laugh, to keep things light, but her heart prevented that, lodged in her throat the way it was.

His eyes heated and his voice lowered as he bent in close to whisper in her ear. "Actually, that wasn't teasing. I meant that. You're still beautiful."

Little flickers of heat danced up and down her arms. His voice was soft, seductive, but not like Charming Max. Like New Max. The guy she really liked. The guy who had waves of masculinity rolling from him over to her. He didn't even have to touch her to send her senses reeling.

She sucked in a breath. Said what needed to be said. "We're not supposed to flirt."

"Really? I like to flirt with you."

He liked to flirt? She longed to flirt. But it was wrong. And they both knew it. "I thought we agreed not to pursue this?"

He grinned at her. "I didn't agree to anything."

The little tingles skipping along her skin heated up. He stepped in closer and she had to fight to hold back a shiver.

"When I told you I was attracted to you, I thought the feelings weren't reciprocated. So I was giving you an out. Now that I know that you like me too, the out is no longer valid."

She gaped at him. "This isn't a game!"

"Why not?"

"Because…" Heat suffused her and she suddenly couldn't remember why. Then Trisha splashed into the pool. "Because of Trisha!"

Gwen picked that exact second to walk over to them, her wet hair combed off her face and a towel wrapped around her black bathing suit. She frowned at Kate, then caught Max's arm. "I'd like to talk to you."

Max held up his whistle. "Can't. I'm lifeguard."

Gwen turned to a gaggle of moms standing on the other side of the pool and called, "Annette?"

Pretty in her scarlet swimsuit, Annette scrambled over. Yanking the whistle from Max's hand, Gwen said, "Be lifeguard for a few minutes."

Annette said, "Sure."

Gwen caught Max's arm and casually led him away.

Kate stood there aghast. Max's mom might have changed

some, but she still loved giving orders. Annette might have to comply. Max might comply out of respect, but Kate had no intention of being bullied.

Furious, she strode into the house and back to the den. Before she reached the door, she heard Gwen say, "I want to find Chance."

She stopped dead in her tracks. She hadn't thought far enough to wonder what Gwen had wanted to talk to Max about, but finding Chance? Was she nuts? Chance had been the reason Max began drinking. Did she want to send him back to the bottle?

Max growled, "What?"

"I never asked you what you and your dad fought about the day Chance left. Since it caused him to run away, I'm guessing it was something about him. Probably something about his real parents. Maybe they were in jail. Maybe one of them was even a murderer." She sighed. "I always assumed you didn't want to find Chance because whatever it was about his parents that you don't want me to know, you believed it would bring trouble to our door."

Fear for Max flooded Kate. She switched to the other side of the corridor, flattening herself against the wall so she could see inside the den, but couldn't be seen.

Max eased back on the sofa, his voice perfectly calm when he said, "That's not exactly right, but close."

"I've decided I don't care. I want my son back. Whatever trouble there is in his past, I believe we can deal with it. But I also respect your judgment enough to know that if you've kept this secret for almost a decade, it must be something you believe we can't deal with. So I've come up with a compromise. Tell me the reason Chance left, what you discovered in his past that was so bad that he ran away when he heard it, and we'll make the decision about whether to bring him home together."

Kate nearly slid down the wall she was leaning against. How the hell was he going to tell his mom that Chance was her husband's biological child from an affair? How did a son find himself in the position of having to tell his mom her husband had cheated? Why hadn't fate forced Brandon to be the one to make the admission? Why did it keep pummeling Max?

A sudden urge to be in the room, to support him, swamped her. But before she could move, Max quietly said, "And if I don't?"

"If you don't tell me, I'll call our attorney tomorrow, instructing him to hire a private investigator."

"That's not much of a choice."

"I know. But, Max, I miss my son." Gwen rose and walked to the wet bar. "Surely after meeting Trisha, you can understand that." Without hesitation, she took a bottle of whiskey from the shelf and poured herself two fingers.

Kate's heart pounded in her chest and tears filled her eyes as she watched Max. It was almost as if his mother was trying to push him so far he drank. Or taunting him. Or totally oblivious to his feelings—which had been the crux of his problems when they were younger. His parents used him, trotted him out for public functions and ignored him when they didn't need him.

It had seemed his relationship with his mother had changed, but maybe it hadn't.

"I tolerated your father not telling me what you argued about only because we already had a bad marriage. It took every ounce of my focus and concentration to be a good wife to that man. I didn't need to hear something about Chance's biological parents that might have made our lives totally intolerable."

Her heart galloping, her breathing painful, Kate could only stare as, totally silent, Max studied his mother. Seconds ticked off the clock as Gwen sipped her whiskey. Max's gaze stayed stuck on her as if he were transfixed.

Suddenly he said, "I'll find Chance." Then he rose and walked to the wet bar.

For Kate the whole scene seemed to happen in slow motion. She felt the weight of every one of his steps as he strode to the bar. Part of her nearly leaped into the room to stop him. The other part watched in horror as he picked up the bottle of whiskey.

The word No! screamed inside her head.

But he slid around the bar, returned the bottle to its place on the shelf and opened the small refrigerator. He lifted out a pitcher and poured himself a glass of iced tea.

Her poor heart had about exploded with fear, and her shimmering nerves struggled to settle down, but she stayed rooted to the spot, feeling things for Max she didn't want to feel. Pride mostly. But also love. This guy did what he had to do. He didn't run. He didn't hide. Not even in a bottle.

Gwen said, "Do you have the resources to find Chance?"

"I can talk to Waterman as easily as you can."

"You think you're going to get to Chance first and tell him not to tell me whatever it was about his parents that caused him to run away."

Max held his mother's stare. "Do you want to know the trouble with Chance's bloodline or do you want him back?"

"If that's the choice you're giving me, I want Chance back."

With that she returned to the bar. She set her glass in the sink, walked over to Max and kissed his cheek. She said, "Thank you, Max," pivoted and headed for the door.

Not wanting to get caught, Kate raced into the small powder room nearby, hiding while Gwen walked by.

When she knew Gwen was gone, she eased out and found herself face-to-face with Max, who was walking up the hall, leaving too.

Stopping, he didn't question her being there, simply said, "My mother is the only person I know who can thank me for buckling under to her blackmail."

Kate couldn't help it. She laughed.

With a sigh, he motioned to the den again. "Have a minute?"

She licked her suddenly dry lips. He wanted to confide and she wanted to be his confidante. It was dangerous territory, but staring into his blue eyes, seeing nothing but a good, honest man—not their past, not the old Max, just a guy she really liked who needed her—she couldn't refuse. "Sure."

Max walked to his desk and fell into the tall-backed leather chair. He leaned back and rubbed his fingers across his eyes. "She wants me to find Chance."

Kate crossed to the desk and sat on the chair in front of it. "Will you?"

Max snorted a laugh. "I said I would. I will."

Was it any wonder she longed to be close to him? He kept his word. He knew his responsibilities. He was exactly the kind of man she wanted to be in love with. And she knew he wanted her. Was she crazy to be afraid of this?

"Maybe everything will be okay when he comes home."

"Right. He was as angry with me for not telling him what I'd discovered as he was with Dad for lying all these years."

"He wanted you to tell him something you considered to be only office gossip?"

Max sighed. "He was eighteen. He was stubborn and bossy." He shook his head. "I can't even imagine what he's like now."

"What do you think he's been doing for the past ten years?"

"Well, when he was in high school, he worked construction on our buildings in the summers. He'd also interned a bit in the offices in the winter." He shrugged. "He had plenty of skills to support himself."

"So you think he's okay?"

He looked at her across the desk. "I wouldn't be able to live with myself if I thought he was alone and hungry."

Of course he wouldn't.

Recognition dawned. "You know where he is, don't you?"

"I know that he's been employed—always employed—for the past seven or so years."

She angled her elbow on the arm of her chair and laid her chin on her open palm. He really made it hard to dislike him. "I should have known."

"I found him after I got sober. The first few years, he had been drifting a lot. He had a few construction jobs, but it was like he didn't have a focus. So I called a guy who called a guy who called a guy, and we found a steady job for him as a construction foreman. He does more than okay."

"That is so sweet."

He bounced out of his chair. "Yeah, well, don't make a saint out of me yet. I've got to get to him through channels, make it look like I didn't have a hand in his life the past six years, then meet him somewhere, and somehow get him to see that he has to come home, and when he does he can't tell Mom her late husband was his real father."

Smiling at his assessment, she rose too. Slowly. Her eyes followed him as he walked around the desk until he was in front of her.

Shirtless, in swimming trunks, bronzed from the sun, he was about as sexy as a man could get. But the serious look on his face was really what drew her. He didn't underestimate his trouble or overestimate his abilities. He also didn't brag about doing good. He just did it.

"Don't look at me like that."

She smiled. "Like what?"

"Like I'm the savior of the world. I'm not. I'm just a guy who picks up pieces."

"You wouldn't have done that eight years ago."

"Eight years ago I was the guy making the pieces. And I'm one drink away from being that guy again." He paused, caught her shoulders and forced her to look at him. "Remember that."

"I do remember that."

He shook his head. "If you did, you'd be running right now, not looking at me like you want to kiss me."

Regret caused her to take a step back. "So you're back to not wanting us to have a relationship?"

"Everything I said today out by the pool I said out of a false belief that my life is different. My mother just reminded me that it's not."

He sounded tired and alone. Like a guy who bore the burden of a dysfunctional family all by himself and had nothing to show for it but the satisfaction that everyone under his care was okay.

She stepped closer, said the words he needed to hear. "No matter what you think, you're a good guy."

He snorted a laugh.

So she stepped closer still. "You'd better accept it this time because if you make me take another step, we're going to be bumping into each other."

His eyes shifted. The burden of duty and responsibility became a light that seemed to glow from inside his soul. A light that called to her. He needed her and she wanted to be needed, to help him, to support him.

Even though he didn't argue, she took the step. The light in his eyes flared, igniting a flickering flame low in her belly. There was never any denying that she was attracted to him, but now…now, all kinds of new emotions were bubbling up in her. She loved this strong, sensible, sane, sexy man.

His voice was quiet, raw when he said, "Don't start something you can't finish."

She swallowed, taking the step she'd never thought she'd take. "How do you know I can't finish it?"

"You told me before you didn't want to finish it."

"Maybe I've changed my mind."

In a flash his hand was at her nape, under the thick waterfall of hair, smoothing along her sensitive skin, sending prickles of excitement careening through her. His other hand fell to her waist. That hand drew her closer as he positioned her head so he could kiss her.

His lips met hers, soft and warm, but not light or easy. The first brush became a press that morphed into something like hungry nibbles that forced her to open her mouth to be able to match him move for move. His tongue swiped inside her mouth, tripping her up, confusing her as lightning flashed inside her head and thunder rumbled through her veins.

But just as quick and fiery as the kiss began, it ended when he pulled away so fast she almost fell.

"I've changed a lot, Kate. I'm older now. Smarter. But in some ways my life's still a mess. I don't need a friend and I don't need just sex. I need a companion. Someone who really can stand by me. Somebody who won't just warm my bed, she'll share my life. All of it. Make damned sure you can do that before you offer what you just offered again. Because I won't let you go a second time."

CHAPTER ELEVEN

As he strode out of the study, Kate ran her trembling fingers over her mouth. If she'd harbored even one iota of doubt about Old Max or their past, that kiss had totally obliterated it.

But she understood what he was saying. If they loved each other, they had to stop playing silly games. But how could they know that they loved each other after eight short weeks? And if he didn't give her time to experiment a bit, would they ever know?

When she stepped outside again, the kids from the playdate were gone. She rounded up Trisha and said goodbye to Annette and Gwen before turning to Max. Running the net through the pool to clean it, he faced her slowly. His eyes still flared with heat, passion. But it was what he'd said that stuck with her. Make damned sure this is what you want. Because I won't let you go a second time.

It tightened her tummy, made her heart beat funny, made her breath stutter…but not in a bad way. In a good way. She knew exactly what he was saying. He wanted her to make the kind of commitment that she couldn't have made as an inexperienced coed and he hadn't been able to make as a charismatic, but tormented son. He wanted her to love him. The real him. Good looks, troubles and all.

She skirted away, one hand on Trisha's shoulder to guide her to their car. Inside, she instantly turned on the air conditioner trying to lower the temperature in her bloodstream, but it was no use. He hadn't just turned her on; he'd offered what she wanted.

Now that she was older and wiser, she knew life wasn't about marrying the richest guy in town and living happily ever after. Life rarely went that smoothly. What she genuinely wanted—what every woman really wanted—was a real life with a real man who knew life sometimes came with trouble, but who also knew how to handle it.

But even considering all that, one thought overshadowed everything. If she discounted the Max she knew, then she'd only known this Max for two months. That wasn't really enough to make a commitment.

"Daddy said we can swim again next Sunday."

"Did he?" Next Sunday was the date she'd planned to return to Tennessee. Instead of leaving, would she be planning to stay…forever?

Was it fair of Max to ask that of her? So soon?

Or was it as he'd said…that she'd made the offer?

She had been the one to step close.

Oh, Lord, she was so confused!

Monday afternoon when he came for his scheduled time with Trisha, Kate eased him and Trisha out the door, suggesting they go for ice cream or go to the park or even the mall. He didn't give her the deer-in-the-headlights look he might have given her when he'd first met his daughter. Instead, he seemed perfectly comfortable. As if he would enjoy his time alone with their daughter, and he definitely wasn't going to push her about the other things.

He confirmed that assumption when he brought Trisha home at around four. He thanked her for letting him have Trisha that afternoon, kissed Trisha goodbye and walked to his car.

But she stood by the door, watching him leave, longing to be able to ask him to stay. Longing to leave with him.

The yearning was so strong that night that she called him. She didn't have his cell number, only the old landline number for their house. Surprisingly, it not only rang, but Max answered.

"Hey."

"Hey." Pleasant surprise colored his voice.

"I, um…" Ah, damn it. She'd planned so many good excuses for why she'd called him and now all of them seemed stupid, phony. She sucked in a breath. Since there was no pretense between them, might as well cut right to the chase. "I've been thinking about what you said on Sunday."

"And?"

"And I think it's too soon for us to make a commitment."

He laughed. "What do you want to do? Date?"

"Lord, that would be awkward."

"Maybe not." His voice softened, warmed. As if he'd realized they needed to compromise. "We've got to start somewhere, Kate."

Her heart pitter-pattered. They were making the decision. They were saying yes. Maybe not to remarriage, but to dating—a step toward remarriage. Suddenly everything that involved—family and friends and…Tennessee (she had a whole life in Tennessee)—seemed to sit on her shoulders like a lead weight.

Then he said, "And we'd have to explain overnight visits to Trisha. Unless you wanted to sneak away for afternoons."

Everything inside her turned to heat and need. Her poor job didn't hold a candle to Max.

When she didn't reply, he laughed. "All right. Maybe it's too soon to be suggesting overnight visits."

But she still couldn't speak. She'd never simultaneously

wanted something and feared it. Especially something that came with such big consequences if they failed.

"So, I set a time to meet Chance."

That brought her voice back. "You did?"

"Yes. I'm flying out to see him on Friday. Interestingly, he lives right in your backyard."

"My backyard?"

"Tennessee."

She laughed. "No kidding."

"So if you'd like to fly out with me… Go visit your friends or your office. Or get some extra clothes. That would be fun."

It would be fun. And if she planned on staying, she'd need those extra clothes. "I could pick up some sweaters from my townhouse."

"Should we leave Trisha behind?"

Her chest tightened. Leave Trisha? And end up making love on his plane? Or in her townhouse? "I think it would be nice for her to see her friends too."

"Good."

She took a breath, glad that he wasn't pressing her. "Good." It felt good. It seemed good. But did she really know what she was doing?

When Max arrived to pick her up Friday morning, Kate was surprised to see him in jeans and a T-shirt. Though she and Trisha wore casual, comfortable clothes, she thought he'd be wearing a suit and tie. Trisha was going on a playdate and she was only taking a stroll through her townhouse, gathering some sweaters and straightening up. Max was about to meet the brother he hadn't seen in ten long years. Surely, he wanted to look better than this?

In his car on the way to the airport, she was tempted to ask, but anything that had to do with Chance was always risky. Though Trish looked to be innocently sitting in the backseat, twisting and turning poor Rachel's voluminous hair, a mother never knew if her child was listening. Worse, she never knew what that child would choose to repeat.

When they got into the plane, and Trisha decided to sit in between her and Max, she again didn't question him. But after they'd dropped Trisha at her friend Teagan's house, when Max stopped his rental car in front of her townhouse and asked if he could come in to change his tennis shoes for boots, she couldn't hold back any longer.

Walking up the sidewalk to her front door, she asked, "Just where are you meeting your brother?"

Max followed her into the foyer. "He's at a construction site. It's Friday. He's still working."

"And you're going to Chance's job site to see him?" Her eyes narrowed.

He sat on one of the stools in front of her cherrywood kitchen island that doubled as a counter for eating cereal and snacks, and slid a foot into a boot. "I have permission from the foreman."

The funny feeling in her stomach grew into a suspicion. "He doesn't know you're coming, does he?"

Max slid into the second boot. "Nope."

"Oh, Max! Are you sure that's a good idea?"

"I have a brother who changes jobs every time he thinks I've found him. And I need to talk to him." He caught her gaze. "I can't take the chance that he'll run before I can talk to him."

"How do you know he won't run when he sees you?"

"Because he's not an idiot. He's just mad. Once he sees me, he'll grudgingly give me a few minutes." He tied his second boot. "That's all I need."

Kate blew out her breath. She understood what he was saying, but her instincts told her he didn't have this situation pegged as well as he thought he did. She glanced around at her townhouse. It needed dusting, but little else, and she made her decision.

"I'm coming with you."

"Kate—"

"He knows me, too, Max. And he's not mad at me. Maybe you could use that to your advantage."

He rose from the stool. "It's possible, but the construction site is almost an hour away from here. I expect to talk to him at least an hour. Then it's another hour to come back to get Trisha. That will take your whole visit. I don't want to ruin your visit."

She shrugged. "I don't mind."

"You're sure?"

Gazing into his perfect blue eyes, she knew she'd do anything for him and maybe it was time for her to admit that. "I'm sure."

He shook his head. "You're crazy. We have absolutely no clue what Chance will be like. But if you want to go, I'd appreciate the buffer you'll probably provide."

They drove forty minutes along the Tennessee Interstate, then another twenty minutes through the countryside until they reached a small town with a community of townhouses on the outskirts.

Surprised, Kate turned to Max. "I thought he was at work."

"He is. He works for a small construction company that does a lot of home repair."

She said, "Oh," just as they turned onto another street. At the end sat two big Dumpsters. Assorted trucks, most bearing the name Turner Construction, were parked around them. The front door of a townhouse was open and two men stood at the hood of one of the trucks, blueprints spread out in front of them.

Max pointed. "That's Josh Turner. He owns this outfit. It took me two days to track him down and find Chance."

They got out of the rental car and Max headed for the two men. He extended his hand to the first man, "I'm Max Montgomery."

"Josh Turner." After dismissing the man beside him with a nod, he thrust out his hand to take Max's. "Great to meet you, Mr. Montgomery."

"This is my ex-wife, Kate."

Josh shook her hand. "Good to meet you." He faced Max again. "Chance is in the house. I'll give him a shout."

With that he left and headed for the front door. On the top step of the stoop, he called, "Hey, Chance! You've got a visitor."

Kate stepped back. She knew construction. She knew shouting was the normal form of communication. But she still winced. Chance had no idea it was his brother he'd see standing in front of the truck. And after he'd stayed away for ten years and disappeared every time he thought Max had found him, she couldn't believe this was going to be a happy reunion.

Josh returned to the truck. "We're totally gutting the place," he explained to Max with a nod at the townhouse. "It'll be a peach when we're done."

"Good bones," Max said, agreeing with him.

Just then a tall, thin man came out of the townhouse. Lanky, as Max had been ten years ago, with thick dark hair like Max's, and blue-gray Montgomery eyes, this had to be Chance.

He approached them, his easy strides displaying the same effortless sexuality that Max had. His smile was slow but powerful, tugging at his full lips and lighting his eyes. "What's up?"

Josh simply stepped back, so that Chance could get a good look at Max.

He stopped. His eyes narrowed. "Max?"

Max stepped forward, as if meeting him halfway. "Chance."

Chance's mouth dropped open. He turned to Josh. The same blue eyes that had sparkled with warmth now glittered with anger. "This is what you called me out for?"

Josh shrugged innocently.

Chance gurgled in disgust. "Do you know who this is?"

Confused, Josh said, "Your brother?"

"The brother I haven't spoken to in ten years!" He shook his head angrily, then looked at the heavens. "I should fire you."

Josh's mouth fell open. "Fire me!"

Max stepped forward. "Come on, Chance. This was all me. I found Mr. Turner. I asked him to set up a meeting."

"Yeah, well, I don't want to meet with you."

Chance turned and trotted down the sloping yard, stopping at a motorcycle innocently parked on the street. He slid on, started it up and was gone so quickly Max, Kate and Josh stood frozen.

Max cursed.

Josh shook his head. "I thought he'd be happy to see you."

"There's a bit of bad blood between us."

"I suspected as much if you needed a third party to set up a meeting, but I still thought he'd be happy." He shook his head again. "He needs somebody in his life. He's such a loner."

"Yeah, he always has been."

"But he's smart." He caught Max's gaze. "Really smart. This time last year he was working for me. Now he's the one buying the older townhouses and renovating them. Rumor has it he's made a bundle. But he's so alone. I was actually relieved when you called me and told me you were his brother. Now there'll be hell to pay on Monday. That is, if he even shows up. As the house's owner, he can handle his part of the job long-distance."

"Great."

Josh combed his fingers through his hair. "Sorry."

"Yeah. Me, too."

With a quick, jerky motion, Josh rolled up the blueprint. He turned and walked up the sidewalk into the townhouse.

Kate looked at Max. "So do we wait around until Monday and see if he comes back?"

"He won't be back."

"You're so sure?"

"He hates me. I always thought it was because I knew about Dad and didn't tell him, but after ten years—" He heaved out a breath. "There's gotta be something I don't know. And that he's not telling."

They drove to Kate's home in silence. Trisha pouted a bit about not wanting to leave, but once the plane was in the air, she fell asleep.

Kate sat on the seat beside Max. "I'm sorry."

"It certainly wasn't your fault." He smiled slightly and put his arm around her, pulling her close. "But thanks. It's nice to have somebody to talk to again."

She snuggled into his chest. "Oh, I'm sure you have lots of people to talk to."

"Sure. Vice presidents talk about their divisions. My mom talks about her garden club. Annette tells me about her kids and lets me vent a frustration or two. But no one really talks about me."

She nestled closer. "You can talk about you all you want with me."

He laughed. Slid his hands down her back and then up again. Sweet peace resonated through him. He'd never thought he'd see her again, let alone have the chance to touch her. Let alone have her in love with him again.

But she was. He could feel it. Sense it. See it in her smile and the way she treated him.

He thought about seducing her right then and there, but Trisha slept peacefully beside them. They talked some more about Chance, but avoided the subject once Trisha awoke.

Bone-tired, he drove them home. When they got into the foyer, Bev instantly hustled Trisha upstairs. "You two say good-night. This child has had a long day and it's time to get her into bed."

Kate said, "Thanks, Mom," as Bev and Trisha disappeared down the upstairs hall. Then, without any warning, Kate stood on her tiptoes and lightly brushed her lips across Max's.

Attraction ricocheted through him as arousal pinged low in his belly. He'd so badly wanted to leave Trisha behind for the Tennessee trip. He'd wanted time alone with Kate. Not to seduce her, to let it happen naturally. Because once they were alone, he was sure it would. But she'd clearly been afraid, and he'd accepted that. But not happily.

So when she kissed him, he kissed her back, packing every ounce of pent-up longing into the movement of his lips across hers, reminding her they were good together and that she shouldn't be afraid. When they finally separated, they were both breathing heavily.

"We're going to have to do something about this, you know."

She walked her fingers up the front of his T-shirt. "Well, I was thinking maybe I could come over tonight." She caught his gaze. "By myself."

Everything inside him stilled. "Really?"

"I think we're ready for some adult time together."

Relief tumbled through him. "Yes, we definitely need some adult time."

"So I'll come over after Trisha is asleep."

"What are you going to say to your parents?"

She frowned. "I don't know." Then she laughed. "Wow,

this is worse than trying to sneak out with you when I was nineteen."

He chuckled, caught her hand and kissed her fingers. She didn't need his help with her parents. She'd be fine. He stepped away reluctantly, letting go of her hand by fractions of an inch. "I'll see you in about an hour, then."

She smiled and headed for the stairway. "I'll see you in about an hour."

He said, "Okay." But he didn't leave. He watched her walk up the steps, then turned to the front door. Walking by the living room he noticed the pocket doors were open. Glancing up from the baseball game he was watching, Dennis saw him.

Rather than pretend he hadn't noticed, Max ducked inside. "Who's winning?"

"Pirates."

"Well, that's a welcome change."

Dennis laughed and Max pointed at the door. "I guess I'll go."

Dennis said, "Okay." Then he shook his head. "No. Stay a second."

Dennis had never been a fan of Max's. But lately they'd been getting along fairly well. So the request that he stay didn't surprise him.

Dennis pointed at the chair beside his. "Have a seat."

Max sat.

"I'd offer you a beer but right now neither one of us is allowed to have one."

Max couldn't help it; he laughed.

"Hum. You think that's funny?"

He shook his head. "I thought it was funny the way you said it. I don't think my drinking was funny."

"And you're really sober now?"

"As a judge."

Dennis laughed. "Oh, don't say that in this county. We're not exactly known for our reputable judges."

"Okay, then let's just say I'm sober."

"Forever?"

"I can't promise forever."

"No, you can't," Dennis said, looking Max in the eye. "And maybe that's something you'd better remember before you go making promises to Kate again that you can't keep."

CHAPTER TWELVE

KATE DRESSED CAREFULLY for her evening with Max, for once not nervous or afraid. She had such strong feelings for him that she was tired of fighting them. She knew he was tired of fighting them too. But she'd also thought of another reason they should sleep together. If they held back on having sex until they were sure, then want of sex could easily lead them into a bad decision, push them into saying and doing things before the time was right.

So she slid into pretty blue panties and a matching lace bra. Then shimmied into a pale blue sundress. With straps that were nothing more than string and a short skirt, the dress certainly showed off the nice tan she'd gotten swimming with Max and Trisha.

She walked down the stairs, then called back to the kitchen, "Hey, Mom! Trisha's asleep. I'm going to the mall."

"The mall!" Her mom called back. "It's almost nine."

"I know. I just need a few odds and ends." She winced. Luckily, she actually was going to the mall before she went to Max's or she'd hate herself for the lie. But since she was popping into the mall, there was no lie. Conveniently leaving off the time she'd return, she grabbed the doorknob and let herself outside.

This late on a summer night, the mall wasn't busy. She

grabbed the few supplies she needed, rushed out and headed for Max's house. Getting out of her car, she realized her cheeks were flushed and her hands were clammy. She hadn't slept with anyone since she'd left Max eight years ago and she didn't want to disappoint him.

At his front door, she sucked in a breath and then rang the bell.

It took a few seconds before he answered. He'd obviously showered. The jeans and a polo shirt he wore were clean. His eyes took a quick trip down her dress to her legs, and darkened.

He said, "You look great." Then he yanked her into his arms and kissed her.

When he finally pulled away, she breathlessly said, "Oh, this old thing."

He laughed, then swept her to him again. This time when he kissed her, she just relaxed. She knew everything she needed to know about Max. She loved him. She trusted him. They were on the verge of forever.

She knew it in her heart and her soul.

But he pulled away again, his eyes dark and stormy. "I'm not sure this is the right thing to do."

Nerves sat on her skin like freckles. The fact that he was having second thoughts didn't scare her. Even deciding to consider getting back together was a huge step. But she was sure. More sure than anything she'd ever thought in her entire life. She'd left him because he drank. Because he lied. Because he connived. He did none of those things now.

She smiled into his eyes. "What? You'd rather play cards?"

He laughed and she stood on her tiptoes and kissed him. As if she'd tripped a switch, he returned her kiss, mating their tongues, letting his hands glide down her bare back, along her arms.

But he suddenly released her again. This time he stepped away. "No." He shook his head as if tormented by demons from hell. "No. This isn't right."

Her heart beat out a frantic rhythm. "Of course it's right."

He took another step back. "Kate." He drew in a breath, shook his head again. "I changed my mind."

Her galloping heart slammed to a halt. "About me being here tonight or about—" She swallowed. "Us?"

"Both."

Disappointment and confusion turned her limbs to jelly. "Why?"

He spun to face her. "Why? For Pete's sake. I'm an alcoholic. You were saddled with me once. Do you really want to be saddled with me again?"

"I wouldn't consider it 'being saddled' when the guy in question works as hard as you do. I wouldn't consider it 'being saddled' when that same guy confides in me, values my opinion and respects me."

"And what if I start drinking again?"

"You won't."

"Really? You know that?"

She licked her lips, suddenly understanding what he needed to hear from her. "Actually, I do know that."

But instead of smiling, his face contorted with anger. "You can't know that! Hell, even I don't know that!"

"I trust you!"

He put his head back and squeezed his eyes shut. "How can you trust me when I'm not supposed to trust myself? Every day is a battle. And the day I let my guard down is the day I could drink again." He shook his head. "You're looking for something that you're not going to get from me and today I realized I have to be honest with you and tell you that."

She narrowed her eyes at him. That didn't make any sense.

If they didn't count the meeting with Chance, they'd had a wonderful day. "What are you talking about?"

"Forever. You want forever. I can't promise you forever." He walked to the refrigerator, pulled out the lemonade, poured himself a glass. "Your dad reminded me of that today."

"My dad?"

"Yes. Come on, Kate. He's not blind or deaf. We were kissing and talking right outside his door. Only an idiot wouldn't have drawn some conclusions, and today he reminded me that I can't promise you forever. Because I can't promise myself forever."

Her heart froze. Her brain felt as if it had melted. She couldn't make sense of any of it. Because none of it made sense. "I'm not sure what you mean."

"I mean that this is wrong. Us." He leaned against the kitchen island. "Go home. Go back to Tennessee. I will see Trisha a few times a year. You can be with us when she visits or my mom will be with us or I'll call Annette."

Her heart simultaneously warmed with love for him and melted with sorrow for him. "Oh, Max."

He swallowed. "Go. Really."

Her eyes filled with tears. She knew what he was saying. She'd basically faced this fear herself. But her dad had confronted him, and he'd responded the way he should. With admissions. He could not say he'd never drink. He could not promise her forever.

She headed for the door. She could tell he wasn't open to help right now, but she would fix this. Somehow or another, she would fix this. "I'll see you tomorrow."

"No!" He sucked in a breath, shook his head. When he spoke again his voice was calmer. "I think we need a break." He turned to return the pitcher to the refrigerator. "Go home. Back to Tennessee."

Hand on the doorknob, she squeezed her eyes shut. But she didn't let her hope wane. Tomorrow they would talk about this again. In the morning, he'd wake up, see that he'd over-reacted and call her.

But he didn't call the next morning. He didn't call at noon. He didn't come over that afternoon. Or the next. Or the next. And when she called him, he wouldn't take her calls. When she went to Montgomery Development, he wouldn't see her. When she went to his house, he wasn't home.

Fury and fear bounced around in her stomach until she thought she would throw up. Her mom took a confused Trisha to the mall. And suddenly she found herself alone with her dad.

"You and I need to talk," he began.

Normally, she would have remembered her dad had had a stroke a few months ago and handled this much better. But the tone of his voice set her teeth on edge. "Why? So you can poke into my life a little more? Maybe you'd like to ruin my relationship with Trisha, too."

He sighed and shook his head. "The man's an alcoholic."

"He's recovering."

"But not recovered." He shook his head again. "Why put yourself in that kind of trouble?"

Her chin rose. "Because I love him."

"He's always been able to charm you."

"He's never once tried to charm me since we've been home. You don't know him."

"You don't know him!"

She grabbed her purse and headed for the door. "I know enough that I'm not going to let you ruin this. I'm going to fix this!"

"And there it is. You're going to fix this."

She stopped.

"Are you turning into his enabler again?"

All the blood froze in her veins. She dropped her purse to the counter.

"You can't go to him. You can't fix this. Only he can."

Kate spent the rest of her visit waiting for Max to call her or come over. He didn't. The days went by slowly, like water dripping from an old faucet. Finally, with only one day left before she needed to be at work, she booked a flight for herself and Trisha. He wasn't going to fix this. Maybe he didn't know how. But her dad was right. She couldn't do this. Couldn't go to him. Couldn't promise to make things right. She had to walk away.

Her parents drove her to the airport. She sat in the car, watching out the window. Trisha chattered nonstop and her mother gave silly replies, obviously trying to lighten the mood.

They reached the airport and her dad drove up to the curbside check-in for her airline. He hobbled out and her mom helped Trisha out. He popped the trunk but Kate pushed his hands aside and wouldn't let him lift her luggage.

"I'm fine, you know. Therapy has worked its magic."

She smiled. "Yeah. I know."

"Oh, so you're not mad at me anymore."

She kicked her tennis shoe along the pavement. "I was never mad at you. At first I was angry with Max. Then I got mad at myself for trusting him again. Now I'm just sad."

In truth, her heart was broken but she wouldn't tell her dad that.

"What are you going to do about Trisha?"

She shrugged. "He said he'll visit in Tennessee. We'll see."

He caught her arm. "He will. He's a good guy."

"Just not a guy to marry."

"Not if he can't promise you forever."

She smiled weakly. "Right."

An attendant checked them in, took their luggage. Trisha kissed her grandparents goodbye and Kate kissed her parents goodbye. Then they walked into the air-conditioned terminal.

Halfway to the escalator, Kate stopped, looked behind her. She'd been so sure that New Max was New Max. That he was honest, reliable, confident and strong. She couldn't believe he was letting her go, but as she and Trisha stepped up to the line for security, she knew he was.

He was.

Two weeks later, Max stared at a picture Annette had given him. She'd brought her camera to Trisha's playdate and had not only snapped shots of the kids, she'd also gotten pictures of him and Trisha together. And she'd gotten one of him and Kate.

That was the picture he was staring at.

Letting her go had ripped his guts out. The only thing that made it possible was the knowledge that she deserved better. She deserved to live life not worried that he'd drink, not worried that one day the pressure would get to be too much and he'd climb into a bottle and never come out.

But, oh God, he missed her.

"Hey, boss…" Annette burst into his office. "My son forgot his lunch. I'd tell him just to eat in the cafeteria but he's allergic—" She stopped. Her eyes softened with misery. "If I'd known those pictures were going to cause so much trouble I never would have taken them."

He tossed the picture of him and Kate to his desk. "They're no trouble."

"Right." She sat on the chair in front of his desk. "Want to talk about it?"

"What's to say? I'm a drunk. She can't trust me."

Annette gaped at him. "She said that!"

"I reminded her of that."

She frowned. "You kicked her out?"

"In a manner of speaking."

"Wow, you're a yutz."

"Really? This time next year, I could be living in a gutter somewhere."

"Well, why don't we get all melodramatic?"

He laughed. "Thanks for your support."

"You don't support yourself. Why should anybody else support you?"

He peered over at her. "Because I need it?"

"We all need it." She shook her head. "Sheesh, get over yourself. Do you think any one of us can promise that this time next year we won't be crippled?"

He frowned at her.

"Can any one of us promise we won't be in a car accident?"

He groaned. "Now you're being ridiculous."

"A little. But the truth is you at least know your problem. You know your addiction. You also know how to control it because you do control it. Yet here you sit, letting it rule you again."

"It does rule me."

"No, it doesn't!" She shook her head. "For the past seven years you've ruled it!"

He sucked in a breath. "I'm ruling it now, but marriage is about forever. And you cannot deny that I might not be able to give her that."

Annette blew her breath out with a pfft noise. "None of us is going to live forever."

"Don't make light of this!"

"I'm not making light of this. I'm trying to get you to see

sense. One day at a time you take care of business in your life. I've been watching it for seven years. I'd never say you were cured, but I would say that you have the tools to know how to live. One day at a time."

She rose. "I'm going to take Billie's lunch to him at school."

With that she left and Max rose from his seat. He walked to the window. He thought about the past seven years. Then he thought about the past couple of weeks. How he'd longed for Trisha and Kate. How he'd never once thought of taking a drink to soothe the ache and, if anything, had strengthened his resolve to stay sober.

He did have tools.

Tools to take him through one day at a time.

One day at a time. One step at a time. He could get to forever.

Couldn't he?

Or was it just wishful thinking?

Saturday morning, Kate had decided to sleep in. Her town-house had been nothing but dusty when they'd returned home, so cleaning it had been easy. And though she'd been bringing work home with her every night, playing catch-up, her life was on the verge of being back to normal.

Except for the ache in her heart.

So when her alarm had sounded at seven, she silenced it then rolled over and went back to sleep. For exactly four minutes. Then her doorbell rang.

She tumbled out of bed, yanking up her too-big pajama pants and deciding the matching tank top covered enough that she didn't have to get a robe to answer the door. Her hair was going out in all directions but anybody rude enough to ring a bell at seven o'clock on a Saturday morning deserved what he or she got.

The bell rang again. Not wanting Trisha to wake, she hastened her steps and grabbed the doorknob. Yanking open the door, she said, "What!"

And watched as Max's eyebrows rose. "You're still asleep."

Max?

Max! Her heart exploded with joy, gratitude and every other positive emotion she could think of, then she realized he was probably here to see Trisha and everything that had come to life inside her deflated.

She turned away from the door. Let him walk in on his own. She wasn't going to let her heart get hurt again because she spent too much time looking at how gorgeous he was in dark trousers and a long-sleeved shirt. With his hair all sticking up as though he'd pulled his fingers through it driving through a strange city.

No. She didn't need to remember things or look at him. There was drooling to consider.

She flopped onto her couch.

He dropped a brown bag of something that smelled yummy on her coffee table. "I brought doughnuts."

Her stomach rumbled in response, but she ignored it. "I'm sure Trisha will love them." She straightened on the sofa, rose and started past him. "I'll go get her."

He stopped her by catching her hand. "Not yet. I was hoping for a few minutes alone with you."

Her eyes narrowed.

"I have some things I want to say."

She yanked her hand from his grip and headed for the stairs that led to Trisha's room on the second floor. "I don't think we have anything left to say."

"Well, I thought I'd start off by saying I love you."

That stopped her.

"I still can't promise you forever. At least not in the conventional sense. But as Annette pointed out, some people will be hit by a bus or in a traffic accident this year. Some of them might have promised forever and they'll be reneging on the deal through no fault of their own."

She walked back over to him and just barely kept herself from checking to see if he had a fever. "Was there enough oxygen in your plane?"

"There was plenty. Listen to me." He caught her hand and pulled her down onto the sofa with him. For the first time, she noticed that along with the bag of yummy-smelling doughnuts, he'd brought a briefcase. He flipped the locks and opened it.

She closed one eye and then the other, and popped them both open, trying to awaken herself because the whole situation felt surreal. Part of her wanted to jump into his arms. The other part wasn't entirely sure he was here.

This could be a dream. After all, she'd dreamed about him more than once since she'd been home. And lots of weird things were happening. He was talking nonsense. Briefcases appeared out of nowhere. She could very well be dreaming.

Reaching inside, he pulled out something shiny and handed it to her.

A vase.

She squeezed her eyes shut then opened them again.

Yep. Still a vase. A heavy vase. She took a closer look. Her breath caught. Her gaze jerked to his. "My mom and dad's vase."

"A duplicate. I had Annette find it online."

"You replaced it." Even she heard the sense of wonder in her voice. Her eyes filled with tears. "I didn't think you'd even realize you'd broken it."

He swallowed. "It's not every day a man wakes up to find his wife is gone and her closet is empty."

She stared at the vase.

"I bought it years ago." He caught her gaze. "The day after you left." With a sigh he put his head back and looked at the ceiling. "When I came downstairs that morning, I saw the broken window and the glasses and all the crystal in front of the fireplace. I barely remembered the tirade, but when I saw the empty space on the shelf I knew exactly what I'd done and exactly why you'd left. I wanted to be ready when you came home."

Her heart about melted with despair. She could picture him waiting for her, maybe even watching out the same window she'd watched through for him. "But I never came home."

"Nope. You disappeared."

She faced him, vase in hand. "You could have found me."

"My pride wanted you to come home. That's part of why I went into AA." He pointed at the vase. "I understood that I'd created the straw that broke the camel's back. So I replaced it. But eventually I realized that replacing the vase didn't solve the problem. So I got myself to AA. When you came home, I wanted to be ready for you."

"You quit drinking for me?"

He sighed. "I might have quit for you, but I stayed sober for myself."

He shifted on the sofa, as if debating telling her the rest of the story. She didn't poke or prod, simply sat there. Her heart was in her throat and her pulse had slowed to such a crawl she wondered if she'd faint. He was here. He loved her. He'd brought her a vase. But she refused to jump to any conclusions. He had to say the right words. She would not be an enabler. She couldn't.

Eventually he said, "About three years in, I realized you probably weren't coming back. I handled that information for about a week but that Friday night, I couldn't do it anymore. If you weren't coming back, I wanted a drink. I sat and stared at a bottle of Scotch for hours. I wanted a drink so bad my tongue could already taste it. You weren't coming home, so I thought my efforts were wasted. But in the end, I couldn't do it. I couldn't even open the bottle let alone pour a shot. Let alone actually drink it. That shook me up until I realized why."

Staring at him, she whispered, "Why?"

He shrugged. "My life wasn't a living hell of waking up mornings with a hangover, not remembering what I'd said, who I'd hurt. Even with my dad still nagging me my life was easier. Manageable. I didn't want to drink anymore because I didn't want life to be any harder than it already was. I tossed the Scotch back to the shelf and the next morning I took control of the company away from my dad. I'd already started doing most of his work, but I decided if I was going to do this I was going to do it right."

With tears clinging precariously to her eyelashes she smiled. "You did it right."

"Thanks." He scooted a little closer to her on the sofa. "You know, I didn't say any of that to make you feel bad." He brushed a tear from the rim of her eyelid. "Stopping drinking wasn't as bad as you think."

"I'm not crying for you."

He arched a brow.

"I'm crying for this."

He glanced down at the vase. "I thought that would make you happy."

"It does. It reminds me that deep in there," she said, trailing her finger lightly over his chest, "is a heart of pure gold."

He inhaled slowly as he caught her gaze. "Don't make a martyr of me."

"You're not a martyr. But you are a good man."

He sniffed a laugh. "I try."

She slid a little closer. "Yes. You do."

"So I can promise you a whole lifetime of trying. A lifetime of me staying sober one day at a time."

"Are you asking me back?"

"I'm asking you to remarry me."

A giggle burst out of her as joy overwhelmed her, making her sound like her nineteen-year-old self, the way she'd giggled the day she'd met him. "Really?"

"I don't want a second chance. I want to start over."

If those weren't the right words, she didn't know what words were. She caught his hands. "Me too."

"Really?"

She laughed. Her heart was playing jump rope in her chest. Every fiber in her being wanted to fall into his arms. Yet they were both holding back. "Why are we so bad at this? I love you."

"I love you too."

"And I want to marry you."

"Me, too."

"So?"

"So?"

"So kiss me, you idiot!"

That was all the invitation he needed. He scooped her into his arms and planted his lips on hers. They started off soft and emotional, but when her mouth opened and their tongues began to dance, heat resonated through her. When she'd gone to his house in her little blue sundress, she'd been so afraid. Today there wasn't a fiber of fear in her. She loved him. She needed him. She'd risk a poor sexual performance for the chance to make love to him again.

Anticipating that Trisha had at least thirty more minutes

before she'd awaken, she flattened her hands on his chest, let them roam a bit before heading for the buttons of his shirt.

He pulled away. "Really?"

She nodded. "I think we have twenty minutes before Trisha gets up."

Longing filled him as he lowered her to the sofa. Her hardened nipples poked through the soft material of her pajama top. He'd noticed right off the bat that she was braless. He'd just never imagined it would come in handy so quickly.

And suddenly he felt a tap on his shoulder. Tap. Tap. Tap. Light fingers. Innocent fingers.

He pulled away, glanced behind him.

"Hi, Daddy."

"Hi, pumpkin." He quickly sat up, bringing Kate with him. Without letting go of Kate, he slid his other arm around Trisha and brought her into their circle of embrace.

Intense gratitude replaced the heat that had been surging through his blood. He had them back. Forever now, if he had any say in it, and he did. He always had. He just hadn't known how to take the steps.

"I smell doughnuts."

"What a coincidence. I brought doughnuts."

"Can I have milk?"

"Yes. But first your mom and I want to tell you something." He drew in a breath. "We're getting married."

She blinked. "Can I have two doughnuts?"

He laughed. Children certainly did have a way of keeping a man humble. But on the bright side, her innocent reaction sort of proved she hadn't really known what her parents were doing when she'd tapped him on the shoulder.

Kate rose suddenly. Grabbing the bag of doughnuts, she headed for the kitchen. "Let's make some coffee."

Max followed her. As townhouses went, hers was large,

with a big cherrywood kitchen that opened to the dining room. Trisha sat on one of the stools by the countertop. He sat beside her.

"So much to plan," Kate said, filling her pot with water and pouring it into the coffeemaker.

Watching her, Max smiled. She was braless. Her pants were too big. Her hair looked as though it hadn't seen a comb in days. "Do we want a big wedding or a small wedding? If we go big we're going to have to wait a year. Go small and we could get married next Tuesday."

Trisha opened the doughnut bag and began digging for her breakfast.

Max laughed. "I don't think Trisha cares. She just wants a doughnut."

Kate spun around with a gasp. "Trisha! At least get a napkin."

And Max settled back on his chair. This was what he wanted, what he'd missed for the past eight years. He loved the wonder of ordinariness. It was something he would never take for granted. They weren't ever going to live in his mother's house on the hill. They would stay in the four-bedroom ranch that they'd built for each other. With the pool and Mrs. Gentry.

Kate scrambled over with a napkin for Trisha. She wiped her mouth. "I swear, sometimes I'd think you were three."

Max laughed and pulled her onto his lap. "This is going to be fun."

"We're going to drive you crazy," she warned.

He placed a smacking kiss on her lips. "And I'm going to love every second of it."

They decided not to call their parents, but to tell them in person when they returned to Pine Ward. Max was ready to face Kate's dad head-on. No fear. And Kate was ready to come home. To redecorate the house so it could accommodate kids. Because she didn't think it wise for one child to inherit an empire. Max wholeheartedly agreed with that.

After breakfast they stayed in her townhouse talking about the future as Trisha played with her Rachel doll on the floor in front of the couch. After lunch, they played Scrabble with Trisha. Ordered Chinese for supper.

And when Trisha nodded off, they walked hand in hand to Kate's bedroom, closed the door and started over.

EPILOGUE

Two years later, Kate Hunter Montgomery watched her daughter and husband splashing in the pool. Exhausted, hot, she rubbed her mound of stomach, praying she'd go into labor. Her son had been due to arrive two days before, but in true Montgomery fashion, he'd decided to be late—probably so he could make an entrance that everyone would remember.

She groaned in disgust, but stopped midgroan. Had that been a pain?

It had come and gone so quickly she couldn't tell, but just the thought that she might be in labor lifted her spirits.

"How's it going over there, Big Mama?" Max called, leaning against the edge of the pool as nine-year-old Trisha climbed out and scurried to the diving board.

"Haven't we been over this Big Mama fixation you have?"

"Yeah, but the name just sort of fits."

The French doors behind Kate opened.

"Did I hear him call you Big Mama again?" Gi Gi asked, sidling up beside Kate's chair and slipping off her flip-flops.

"Yes, you did."

"In some states, they shoot men for saying things like that to pregnant wives."

Max burst out laughing and ducked under the water as Trisha landed with a splash.

Gi Gi sighed. "Honestly, I don't know where he gets that silly side of his."

Kate rubbed her tummy. "Oh, sometimes it's fun."

Gi Gi glanced down. "Are you okay?"

Kate sucked in a breath. "I'm not sure, but I think I may have had a labor pain."

Gi Gi's face brightened. "Oh my God."

"Relax. I've thought I was having pains every day this—" She stopped as another pain moved down her tummy. "Okay, that one felt real."

"Really!"

Kate laughed. "You can be all excited because you'll be sitting at the pool this time tomorrow when I'm in heavy labor."

Gi Gi gaped at her. "You think it will take that long?"

She shrugged. "Trisha did."

Removing her cover-up, Gi Gi said, "Second babies don't take as long as first babies." She headed for the pool. "Don't wait too long before you tell Max."

"I suppose this means I need to tell my parents, too."

Gi Gi turned, put her hands on her hips. "Well, you certainly want them there."

She laughed. She did want them there. She wanted her fretting mom and her cool-as-a-cucumber dad. He'd been a little careful about accepting Max back into their family, but Max had been patient and her dad had come around.

Another pain rippled down her tummy. She frowned. Wasn't that a tad close? Maybe she should be timing these?

Gi Gi jumped into the pool. Trisha threw a ball at her and they began batting it back and forth.

A few minutes later, another pain attacked her and this time she groaned. Max was at her side in seconds.

"What's up?"

"I think I'm in labor."

"Okay."

"And the pains are coming too soon and too fast." She groaned again. "Man, am I sorry we don't have a driver."

Lifting her out of the chair, Max laughed. "Now's not exactly the time to get snooty."

"I'm not snooty!" she said, then she moaned. "This baby is coming right now. And I want somebody already in a car! Somebody who knows how to speed through traffic!"

Gi Gi got out of the pool. "Okay. Here's what we'll do. You two go. Trish and I will call your parents. Then we'll get cleaned up and we'll bring fresh clothes for Max."

Kate gratefully said, "Sounds like a plan."

She let Max lead her. After all, that was the only fun men had in this birthing experience. Leading. Watching. Encouraging screaming, agonized wives.

They made it to the hospital with plenty of time to spare. Her parents raced in as if she were dying, not having a baby. Then Gi Gi and Trisha arrived with the clean clothes for Max.

But Kate had another two hours of contractions and then suddenly it was time. Nurses scurried around, repositioning Kate, checking her blood pressure, preparing the space for the doctor.

Dennis excused himself. "I've seen two babies being born. That was enough." He put his hand on Trisha's shoulder. "Frankly, I think you can live another few years before viewing this glorious experience, too."

Her eyes wide, Trisha nodded and followed her granddad out of the room.

Bev said, "Well, I'm staying. I'm not squeamish."

Gi Gi laughed. "Me neither."

Max almost wished he could leave, too. Instead, he settled in on the stool they'd given him. Positioned by Kate's chest, he held her hand. He'd missed Trisha's birth. He wouldn't miss Humphrey's. He winced. "This might be a good time to come up with a new name for the kid."

Kate squeezed her eyes shut as another contraction hit her, then said, "What? You don't like Humphrey?"

"As a name for hippos? I think it's fine. For a baby? No. I do not like Humphrey."

The doctor arrived. He snapped on gloves. "Let's see what we have here." He tunneled in under the sheet that was still around Kate's legs. "Oh, wow."

He popped out. "Things are moving really quickly down here. Let's roll."

And roll they did. Within three minutes the baby was born. It hadn't been as scary or as long as either his mother or mother-in-law had predicted. After a quick wipe and some procedures Max didn't watch, the baby was placed in Kate's arms.

His eyes filled with tears. "Oh my God."

Kate whispered, "I know. Look at him. He's beautiful."

"He's handsome," Max corrected, his voice overflowing with emotion. "And I'll bet he's smart, too."

Bev scooted over. "Wow. He's adorable."

"He's wrinkled and prunelike," Gi Gi said. "But so beautiful that I…" She stopped when her voice broke and she burst into tears. "I'm sorry," she said, then she sniffed and reached for a tissue on the bedside table. "I just…" She swallowed hard and slipped away from Kate's bedside.

With Kate busy doting over the baby with her mom, Max let his gaze follow his mom, who sobbed quietly in the corner. She composed herself and rejoined the group, ohhing and ahhing over the new baby.

From the bottom of the bed, the doctor said, "So what's his name?"

Kate glanced at Max, then up at Gi Gi. "If Max doesn't mind, I'd like you to have the honor of naming him, Gi Gi."

She took a step back, put her hand on her heart. "That is so sweet." Then she burst into tears again.

Bev laughed. "Who'd have thought you'd break down at something as simple as a birth?"

Max hadn't thought it. But he should have. He should have realized this would hit his mom hard. She might not have birthed Chance. But she'd raised him. Hugged him, cuddled him, kissed his cuts and scrapes, helped him with his homework.

Glancing at his own baby boy, he swallowed hard. Come hell or high water, he would get his brother home.

Kate looked at his mom. "So?"

She sniffed. "So I've always been fond of the name Clayton."

Kate smiled, peeked down at her squirming bundle of joy. "Clayton."

"We can call him Clay," Gi Gi suggested.

Bev slid two fingers along the new baby's knuckles. "Clay." She smiled at Gi Gi. "I like it."

Max laughed with relief. "Me, too."

Kate smiled. "Me, too."

And Max relaxed on his stool, enjoying the moment. Their family was so different now. Close. Comfortable with each other. Supportive of each other. There was no worry that he would take a drink. Not because he was foolish enough to believe he was cured, but because he was smart enough to be vigilant. Only a fool would risk this.

The nurses took the baby. The doctor finished up. Bev and Gi Gi kissed Kate's cheeks, both suggesting she get some rest.

Max leaned in and kissed her forehead. "I love you."

She mumbled, "I love you, too."

"You do need to get some rest."

"I could use a week of sleep."

The nurse laughed. "Sorry. You get about an hour before they'll ask you to try to breastfeed."

Max kissed her forehead again. "So you rest and I'll deal

with the thundering horde in the waiting room. When I called Annette she said she was coming. Your mom saw your neighbor Mrs. Mayberry, so we know she's here. And let's not forget Mrs. Gentry."

Kate laughed, but Max could see she was already drifting off.

So he left. He took off the surgical hat they'd put on his head and stuffed it into the pocket of the scrubs they'd told him to wear. As he shoved on the swinging doors that would lead him to the waiting room, a wonderful peace stole over him.

He might have had rough spots. He would definitely have more rough spots ahead of him—especially when he dragged Chance home; and if it killed him, he would. But right at this moment he was the luckiest man in the world.

* * * * *

Mills & Boon® Hardback

September 2012

ROMANCE

Unlocking her Innocence	Lynne Graham
Santiago's Command	Kim Lawrence
His Reputation Precedes Him	Carole Mortimer
The Price of Retribution	Sara Craven
Just One Last Night	Helen Brooks
The Greek's Acquisition	Chantelle Shaw
The Husband She Never Knew	Kate Hewitt
When Only Diamonds Will Do	Lindsay Armstrong
The Couple Behind the Headlines	Lucy King
The Best Mistake of Her Life	Aimee Carson
The Valtieri Baby	Caroline Anderson
Slow Dance with the Sheriff	Nikki Logan
Bella's Impossible Boss	Michelle Douglas
The Tycoon's Secret Daughter	Susan Meier
She's So Over Him	Joss Wood
Return of the Last McKenna	Shirley Jump
Once a Playboy…	Kate Hardy
Challenging the Nurse's Rules	Janice Lynn

MEDICAL

Her Motherhood Wish	Anne Fraser
A Bond Between Strangers	Scarlet Wilson
The Sheikh and the Surrogate Mum	Meredith Webber
Tamed by her Brooding Boss	Joanna Neil

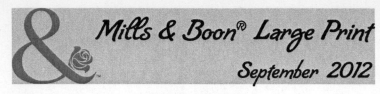
Mills & Boon® Large Print
September 2012

ROMANCE

A Vow of Obligation	Lynne Graham
Defying Drakon	Carole Mortimer
Playing the Greek's Game	Sharon Kendrick
One Night in Paradise	Maisey Yates
Valtieri's Bride	Caroline Anderson
The Nanny Who Kissed Her Boss	Barbara McMahon
Falling for Mr Mysterious	Barbara Hannay
The Last Woman He'd Ever Date	Liz Fielding
His Majesty's Mistake	Jane Porter
Duty and the Beast	Trish Morey
The Darkest of Secrets	Kate Hewitt

HISTORICAL

Lady Priscilla's Shameful Secret	Christine Merrill
Rake with a Frozen Heart	Marguerite Kaye
Miss Cameron's Fall from Grace	Helen Dickson
Society's Most Scandalous Rake	Isabelle Goddard
The Taming of the Rogue	Amanda McCabe

MEDICAL

Falling for the Sheikh She Shouldn't	Fiona McArthur
Dr Cinderella's Midnight Fling	Kate Hardy
Brought Together by Baby	Margaret McDonagh
One Month to Become a Mum	Louisa George
Sydney Harbour Hospital: Luca's Bad Girl	Amy Andrews
The Firebrand Who Unlocked His Heart	Anne Fraser

ROMANCE

MEDICAL

Mills & Boon® Large Print

October 2012

ROMANCE

A Secret Disgrace	Penny Jordan
The Dark Side of Desire	Julia James
The Forbidden Ferrara	Sarah Morgan
The Truth Behind his Touch	Cathy Williams
Plain Jane in the Spotlight	Lucy Gordon
Battle for the Soldier's Heart	Cara Colter
The Navy SEAL's Bride	Soraya Lane
My Greek Island Fling	Nina Harrington
Enemies at the Altar	Melanie Milburne
In the Italian's Sights	Helen Brooks
In Defiance of Duty	Caitlin Crews

HISTORICAL

The Duchess Hunt	Elizabeth Beacon
Marriage of Mercy	Carla Kelly
Unbuttoning Miss Hardwick	Deb Marlowe
Chained to the Barbarian	Carol Townend
My Fair Concubine	Jeannie Lin

MEDICAL

Georgie's Big Greek Wedding?	Emily Forbes
The Nurse's Not-So-Secret Scandal	Wendy S. Marcus
Dr Right All Along	Joanna Neil
Summer With A French Surgeon	Margaret Barker
Sydney Harbour Hospital: Tom's Redemption	Fiona Lowe
Doctor on Her Doorstep	Annie Claydon